She was nervous about meeting Benedikt, and she shouldn't be. He was nothing more than a man with whom she'd struck a deal a lifetime ago.

A marriage deal but still a deal.

It was time to end it, to move on to the next chapter in her life. She wanted a child, someone to love, a family, even if it was one she had to make herself. She wanted someone to share her life. She'd been alone for too long...

She lifted the cup to her lips, desperate for a jolt of the hot liquid, for a hit of caffeine. Being back in Iceland, the first time in forever, had her feeling more emotional and off balance than she'd expected.

She had to pull herself together before she met Benedikt.

"Hello, Millie."

Millie spun around, saw his tall frame standing at the door and tried to replace the cup on its saucer. She missed by a mile and coffee spilt onto the pale hardwood floors and splattered over her boots.

Damn. She'd really been looking forward to that cup of coffee.

Joss Wood

A NINE-MONTH DEAL
WITH HER HUSBAND

HARLEQUIN
PRESENTS

HARLEQUIN® PRESENTS™

ISBN-13: 978-1-335-59314-6

A Nine-Month Deal with Her Husband

Copyright © 2023 by Joss Wood

Recycling programs for this product may not exist in your area.

For questions and comments about the quality of this book, please contact us at CustomerService@Harlequin.com.

Harlequin Enterprises ULC
22 Adelaide St. West, 41st Floor
Toronto, Ontario M5H 4E3, Canada
www.Harlequin.com

Printed in U.S.A.

Joss Wood loves books and traveling—especially to the wild places of southern Africa and, well, anywhere. She's a wife, a mom to two teenagers and a slave to two cats. After a career in local economic development, she now writes full-time. Joss is a member of Romance Writers of America and Romance Writers of South Africa.

Books by Joss Wood

Harlequin Presents

Hired for the Billionaire's Secret Son

Cape Town Tycoons

The Nights She Spent with the CEO
The Baby Behind Their Marriage Merger

Scandals of the Le Roux Wedding

The Billionaire's One-Night Baby
The Powerful Boss She Craves
The Twin Secret She Must Reveal

Harlequin Desire

The Trouble with Little Secrets
Keep Your Enemies Close...

Visit the Author Profile page
at Harlequin.com for more titles.

PROLOGUE

Twelve years ago

'I'M SORRY TO disturb you, but Millie Magnúsdottir is here.'

Benedikt Jónsson looked up to see his late business partner's daughter charging into his office, every muscle in her body taut with tension.

Millie's dyed coal-black hair hung over her shoulders in two fat braids and her light green eyes were heavily rimmed with kohl. 'He's going to charge me with theft and if I get convicted I might end up with a permanent criminal record.'

He'd heard the news this morning from his irate in-house lawyer, who'd spent more time on Millie's escapades than any corporate lawyer should. According to Lars, the night before last, Millie had appropriated her father's Ferrari for a midnight joy ride with her friends.

He wished the teenager would stop looking for trouble. This month alone, she'd been photographed leaving three clubs three nights in a row in the early hours of the morning, carrying her two-inch heels. She'd 'forgotten' to pay for a gold lamé top at an exclusive boutique and was, supposedly, having an affair with a famous Danish drummer twenty years her senior.

Every press article mentioned she was the wayward, uncontrollable daughter of Magnús Gunnarsson, widower of Jacqui Piper, the founder of PR Reliance, the company half owned by Ben. Every time she hit the headlines, for all the wrong reasons, Millie generated bad press for the company and their competitors laughed, delighted. She was an unmanageable PR nightmare.

Ben told Millie to sit, but she ignored him, choosing to pace the area in front of his desk.

'Taking his Ferrari for a joyride was stupid, Millie.'

Why had she taken Magnús's brand-new car? Was she trying to push his buttons simply because that's what eighteen-year-old rebels did? And why was she here, talking to him about it? They'd little to do with each other. He was just her mum's business partner, a guy whom she'd met only a handful of times over the years. Before her death, Jacqui had kept her business and personal life separate.

'Sit down,' Benedikt told her, linking his hands across his stomach and leaning back in his chair. She heard the command in his voice, released an audible sigh and perched on the edge of a chair, a scared bird ready to take flight. Or peck.

'What do you want from *me*?' he asked. He could

try to persuade Magnús from pressing charges, but didn't think it would help. Magnús loved to thwart him: he'd always resented his and Jacqui's close relationship. If Benedikt said something was white, Magnús would insist it was black. Dealing with him since Jacqui's death had been three years of hell. Worse than that, PR Reliance was simply ticking along.

And he was stuck with Millie's father for another seven years because Millie would only take control of her trust fund, and the half-share of PR Reliance she'd inherited, when she turned twenty-five. The thought of dealing with Magnús for another seven weeks, never mind seven years, made him feel ill.

Millie's eyes slammed into his and he saw the determination in hers, and desperation. He'd mourned Jacqui, but his grief was nothing compared to Millie losing her mum at fifteen. Her numerous scandals, each one worse than the last, were surely desperate cries for attention. He didn't know much about teenagers, but he suspected Millie was trying, first by acting out and then by rebelling, to get a reaction, good or bad, from her father.

Benedikt wished she wouldn't. It made his job ten times harder than it needed to be…

'I have a proposition for you,' Millie quietly stated.

This should be good. But whatever it was, he'd have to say no. He didn't make deals with teenagers who were barely adults. No matter how much maturity, determination and sense of purpose he saw in their eyes.

'I want to get married.'

Benedikt blinked, then frowned. She was eighteen, far too young for marriage.

Millie pushed her heavy fringe from her face with a black-tipped finger. 'You're wondering why I'm telling you this. Can I explain?'

Benedikt nodded, disconcerted by the direction of their conversation.

'Magnús is not my real dad,' Millie stated, looking down. Benedikt's attention sharpened even further. What was she talking about?

'Why do you think that?' he asked, keeping his tone even.

'Magnús let it slip during an explosive argument recently. He told me he's glad I don't carry his DNA because I'm a complete embarrassment.'

Beneath her pale foundation, he saw stripes under her eyes and a tension in her mouth no one her age should have.

'He wasn't supposed to tell me, he'd promised my mum he wouldn't, but I think he's relieved I know.'

Ben rubbed his jaw, not sure what to say or do, or how this related to her wish to get married.

'It explains why Magnús and I never got along,' Millie added.

He glanced at his monitor and wished he could get back to work. He didn't understand why she was talking to him about this. He ran the company, he wasn't her confessor.

'I wish I knew why she lied to me and why she never told me who my real dad was.'

The pain in Millie's eyes was tangible, a living, breathing thing, and Benedikt wanted to pull her into his arms, to give her the support she so badly needed. But he didn't know her well enough. She was his dead partner's kid—to her he was the guy who now ran her mum's business. They weren't friends—hell, they were barely more than acquaintances.

But Benedikt did wonder why some people—he and Millie, for instance—won the 'one bad parent' lottery.

'It's obvious Magnús wants me out of his life and I most certainly would like him out of mine,' Millie told him, sounding much older than her eighteen years.

Ben would like Magnús out of his life as well, but he didn't see any way of that happening any time soon. Sadly. Benedikt noticed the gleam in Millie's eyes and recognised it as the same one her mother had when she was hatching a plan...

Danger ahead.

'Magnús has a lover, she's been around for a few years,' Millie stated. 'I'm not sure if their affair started before or after Mum got sick, but he's besotted with her. Or besotted with her money.'

He was aware of Magnús's wealthy lover.

'He wants to move to Italy with her but, per Mum's will, he can't leave Iceland. He has to stick around and look after my interests until I turn twenty-five,'

Millie continued. 'The only way he can leave Iceland, and be rid of me, is if he resigns as my trustee.'

'But that will only happen in seven years,' Benedikt pointed out.

Millie's gaze was steady on his face. 'Or it could happen sooner if I marry,' she stated. 'I looked at her will. If I marry, my husband can take over as my trustee.'

This was another of her crazy schemes and Benedikt felt ice invade his veins. Millie, Reykjavik's wild child marrying?

'That's a crazy idea, Millie!'

She shook her head. 'No, it would work! If I choose the right man and if I made a deal with him.'

He couldn't believe he was having this mad conversation, but Benedikt was intrigued enough by her mature tone and her direct gaze to roll his finger, suggesting she continue.

She leaned back, crossed her legs and folded her arms. 'I think a marriage of convenience would be the way to go and the marriage would be nothing more than a legal document. I want to go to the UK to study, get out of Magnús's life and start a new chapter. I know Magnús will be thrilled to be rid of me. He might even forget about charging me with theft of his Ferrari.'

'Those charges won't stick.' He hoped.

'Maybe not, but it'll be another scandal.'

'You've told me why marrying would work for you and for Magnús,' Benedikt stated, 'but what's in it for the guy who you plan on marrying? He's got a stake in this, too.'

He recognised her sly smile and narrowed his eyes at her. She'd borrowed the smile from her mum and it meant trouble. 'I know you have someone in mind, Millie,' he told her, feeling sorry for her victim.

She nodded. 'I do. He'd get rid of Magnús and be able to run this place without interference, from either Magnús or me. He'd be able to live his life exactly as he did before—we'd both pretend we weren't married and wouldn't impose any conditions on each other.'

Right. *He* was her intended victim. *Gut-punch.*

Millie continued her explanation. 'I want to do an art degree and become a jewellery designer. When I take control of the trust and the shares, in seven years, I'll sell you my half of the business. All you'd have to do was to stay married to me until then.'

By marrying Millie, he would gain complete control of PR Reliance and could implement everything Magnús had vetoed. He could expand, venture into new markets and take some risks he knew would pay off. He'd have freedom in his business life. And, if he was hearing Millie right, in his personal life as well. Since breaking his engagement to Margrét, Ben had had only puddle-shallow encounters with women. He had no intention of marrying, or making *any* type of commitment, to a woman again. Marrying Millie wouldn't cause a ripple in his personal life, but it would reinvigorate his business life.

Once he moved past the shock factor, Benedikt couldn't for the life of him see a flaw in her plan.

Apart from their age difference, it was a no-brainer. But if this was going to be a hands-off, business-only, don't-have-anything-to-do-with-each-other marriage, would the eight-year difference between them matter? She knew what she was walking into, what she wanted from this arrangement.

After allowing him to think for a few minutes, Millie arched her black eyebrows. 'Well? What do you think?'

Benedikt rubbed his jaw before speaking again. 'I have two conditions,' he replied.

Her eyes closed and she shook her head. 'Of course you do,' she muttered. 'I thought I covered all the bases. Why can't anything be simple?' She sighed. 'What is it?'

He allowed a small smile to touch his lips. 'One, you stop hitting the headlines. And, two, you allow me to run PR Reliance without any interference from you.'

'I have no interest in my mum's business, so I'll agree to that. But you've got to promise never to lie to me.'

He far preferred the truth, however hard it was, to dishonesty. The promise was easy to make.

Benedikt pulled a notepad towards him and picked up his fountain pen. It seemed they had a deal to make, a marriage to undertake.

He looked at Millie and nodded. 'Right, let's hammer out the details.'

CHAPTER ONE

Present day...

IN REYKJAVIK, outside the hotel she'd booked last week in the historical heart of the city, Millie left the taxi and icy air burned a path down her throat. Man, it was cold. And, at nearly three in the afternoon, daylight was fast disappearing. She smiled at the driver who'd parked directly outside the entrance and thanked him for collecting her from the airport before turning to thank the harried-looking porter pulling her case from the boot of the sedan.

It was about a hundred degrees below and she buried her nose in her cream scarf as she walked up the steps to the front door of the hotel, wishing she was wearing another four layers of clothing.

Despite only being outside for no more than a minute, she was mind-numbingly, toe-curlingly cold. She managed to stutter a greeting to the doormen and immediately headed for the freestanding fireplace in the centre of the impressive room. She held her hands to the warmth and her fingers started to tingle.

Man, she'd forgotten how far north Iceland was and how cold it could get. Life in London had made her soft.

After defrosting, she peeled her scarf from her neck and undid the buttons on her thigh-length coat. She wore tight jeans tucked into knee-high, stiletto-heeled leather boots and a cranberry-coloured jersey that skimmed her hips and ended at the top of her thighs. She brushed a hand over her long hair, which she'd pulled back into a low tail.

She could murder a cup of coffee...

Draping her coat and scarf over her arm, she looked around the small lobby and her eyebrows lifted. The hotel had more of a feel of a modern country house, with long, comfortable sofas and exceptional art on the walls. There was no reception desk and she wondered where to check in...

'Ms Piper?'

Millie greeted the tall, thin and extremely stressed man who'd addressed her. 'Hello.' She smiled at him and thought he could do with a half-bottle of homoeopathic stress drops.

'I'm surprised to see you here, Ms Piper.'

Piper looked at the name tag attached to his lapel—Stefán, General Manager. Why should he be surprised? She'd made a reservation and she'd arrived. That was the way hotels worked, wasn't it?

A young woman approached them at a fast clip and touched Stefán's arm. 'Sir? Will you come? *Now?*'

Stefán picked up the urgency in his colleague's

voice. 'Ms Piper, will you excuse me?' He pointed to a couch behind her, facing the snowy street. 'I'll be right back, if you'll wait?'

Well, it wasn't as though she had a choice. Millie nodded and watched as he fast-walked across the lobby and disappeared behind a door. She noticed her suitcase standing next to a pot plant and grimaced. She hoped there wasn't a problem with her booking.

Now a lot warmer, Millie took off her coat and sat on the edge of the backless couch and looked at the huge Christmas tree in the corner, white fairy lights its only decoration. Christmas was just three weeks away, but she wasn't overly excited about the holiday.

Without a family, the holiday season was more of a trial than a celebration. Millie placed her chin on her fist and sighed. The last Christmas she truly enjoyed was when she was fourteen, the year before her mum died. She and her mum had decorated their Reykjavik house with greenery and fairy lights and made a wreath for the front door. They'd polished off many hot chocolates and belted out Christmas carols on the piano as snow covered the city. It had been a happy time, mostly because Magnús had been away for most of that December...

At fourteen, she'd believed her mum when Jacqui told her her dad was working, that he was in a different time zone and that's why he couldn't call her. That, despite being unemotional and distant, Magnús definitely loved her.

But she'd still wondered why Magnús never hugged her, why he'd never shown her a hint of the affection her friends' fathers gave them. Magnús didn't show any interest in her, or her life, and, despite her mum's reassurances, she genuinely believed, for the longest time, she was defective and unlovable.

That there was something wrong with her...

Losing her mum had rocked her world and, despite her thinking he couldn't be more distant or emotionally unavailable, Magnús retreated from her life in every way he could. She felt as though she was sharing the house with a stranger, someone who occasionally used the bedroom he shared with her mum.

She'd so desperately wanted his attention, good or bad, so she resolved to make him notice her. She started bunking school, acting out, dressing in weird and alternative clothing styles.

She picked fights and taunted him, wanting to see if she could penetrate his mask of cold disdain. It took him a few years, but his mask finally cracked when she'd taken his car that time. He'd lashed out, calling her a barnacle and a leech, someone he couldn't stand. He'd had to share Jacqui with her and he resented all the attention her mum gave her.

'But I'm your child, too!' she'd protested, feeling as though he'd gutted her with a sharp scalpel.

'You're not mine, thank God! I would hate to think such a useless, snivelling, pathetic creature carried any of my DNA!'

It was one sentence, twenty-one words, but after hearing and digesting them, Millie finally understood his nearly two decades of emotional uninterest. She'd been furious and so hurt but, because she was her mother's daughter, she'd had enough pride to come up with a solution to banish Magnús from her life. And, damn, it had worked well.

Her stepfather was now a distant memory, someone she tried not to think about. But Millie still didn't understand why her mum had lied to her for so long and why she died without telling her the truth. She and her mum had been so close and they'd shared everything. But she would never have known the truth if it weren't for Magnús losing his temper.

Millie couldn't help wondering who her real father was and why her mum had thought it so important to keep his identity a secret. Did he know about her? Did she look like him? Did she have any siblings?

She loved her mum, always would, but damn, sometimes she hated her for leaving her with so many unanswered questions. For leaving her to live with lies, for leaving *her*. Death, the ultimate form of abandonment.

Her mum's death, her secrets and lies and Magnús's uninterest in her, had coloured the rest of her life. Millie found it exceptionally difficult to trust anyone and, while she had friends, she wasn't close to anyone. Nobody knew that behind the semi-famous jewellery designer was a messed-up woman with massive trust and family issues.

There was only one person she trusted fully, only one man who'd never lied to her or let her down—

her husband of twelve years. The one she'd travelled to Reykjavik, unannounced, to see.

Today would be their second meeting. He'd find this one as unexpected as the first and she hoped this meeting would go as well.

When she'd suggested she and Benedikt marry it was a shot-in-the-dark solution, but within a few days Benedikt had a lawyer draw up a prenup and that was it.

They'd hammered out another agreement on his notepad and, despite it not being a legal document, it carried the most weight. Millie easily recalled their terms…their union would be a marriage in name only and Benedikt would not exert any control over her, provided she stayed out of legal trouble and out of the headlines. As her husband and trustee, he had agreed she could use her trust fund to study what she wanted, where she wanted, provided she got a degree, *any* degree. And that he would entertain any other reasonable requests she made for money. They would correspond via email and would live their own, very separate lives.

After she turned twenty-five, they would discuss divorce and Millie agreed to give Ben the first option to buy her shares in PR Reliance International, when he was ready to do so.

Seven years had come and gone, then ten. Magnús had passed on. She didn't go to his funeral and wasn't surprised when he left everything to a lover. And, after studying jewellery design, she'd become a sought-after jewellery designer. Another two years passed and, in name only, she'd been married to Benedikt for twelve years.

Now it was time for them to divorce…

Because, while she never wanted to be married in the usual sense of the word—she had too many trust issues to risk her heart—she *did* want a child. She wanted the close relationship she'd had with her mum with her own child, she wanted to regain the feeling of being part of a team, her and her mum's *it's us against us the world* feeling.

But she was also very tired of being alone. She wanted someone to share her life and a child was a much safer bet than a lover. She could pour her pent-up love into a child. To give it to a lover was far too dangerous.

She'd had relationships and some lasted longer than others. But when her partners started pushing for more, when they started using words like 'love' and 'commitment' and 'taking this to the next level', she always found a reason to call it quits.

Her and Benedikt's marriage was a marriage of convenience and she knew he'd had many, many affairs over the years. Their marriage was need-to-know information and nobody, to date, needed to know. And since the death of Magnús, only she and Benedikt knew they were hitched.

But everything would change, everything *needed* to change, if she brought a new life into the world.

Millie swiped her finger across the screen of her phone and the sperm bank website she'd been looking at earlier populated her screen.

She intended to make full use of technology and have a baby the modern way. Just in case something went wrong down the line, she'd had her eggs harvested and now all she needed was a sperm donor to create her own little family.

Millie was surprised at how many men featured on the sperm bank's database, and the range of diversity, and couldn't decide whom she wanted to be her baby's biological dad. Brains and athleticism were important to her, but, while she'd like him to be handsome, his looks weren't crucially important. She had to make a choice and the baby doctors would do their magic in a laboratory before placing the viable embryos back inside her.

The image of Benedikt flashed on the big screen of her brain and Millie frowned. What made her think of her handsome, but uncommunicative, husband in name only? On paper, he would make a great donor, he was super-smart, very athletic, and, because he'd grown PR Reliance into an international empire and made them both ridiculously rich, she knew he was ambitious and driven. But she didn't know any more about him than she did about the donors on the sperm bank website.

She glared at the screen. She wanted more, she needed the personality quirks of the donors. How would she know if she was choosing a man who was reticent and uncommunicative, narcissistic and selfish? How did she know if her baby's father was outgoing? Or sensitive? Or temperamental?

And that was why she was struggling, the reason

she couldn't make a choice. She didn't much care about eye colour or height, but she did care whether her child was going to inherit its father's fatal flaws. Look, she wasn't perfect, she was emotionally closed down and she struggled to trust and make friends, but she tried to be kind, tried to be a good person.

Millie sighed. Even if she had a donor in mind, she wouldn't allow herself to become pregnant while she was still married to Benedikt, because it didn't seem, or feel, right. She wanted to leave the past, all of her past, full of lies, behind her. Her mum, the person she had loved the most and who had loved her, had lied to her and died without telling her the truth about her biological father. Magnús colluded in the lies because, Millie presumed, he'd loved her mum.

To her, love was twisted, tainted for ever by untruths and deceptions. Honesty was her highest value and she couldn't trust anyone to be completely honest with her. Love, a partnership and raising a child together required transparency and a level of trust impossible for her to reach, or believe in. No, it was better for her to raise a child alone. If she did this alone, she'd never be disappointed, hurt or lied to again.

It was a trifecta of self-protection.

That was why she was here, in Iceland after twelve years. Sending Benedikt an email with a blithe request for a divorce seemed like a cop-out. She felt she needed, at the very least, to have a face-to-face meeting with the man.

Millie looked up at the hotel manager's approach and stood. 'I'm sorry we were interrupted,' he said.

'Not a problem. Is there something wrong with my reservation?'

Stefán rubbed the tips of his fingers across his forehead. 'I take it you didn't get the email we sent yesterday?'

Millie wasn't about to explain she wasn't good at checking her personal emails. She'd skimmed through her mail yesterday, seen a message from the hotel and presumed it was a standard, looking-forward-to-seeing-you letter.

'Our correspondence strongly suggested that, unless it was an emergency, you postpone your trip. We have a blizzard on its way and your plane would've been one of the last to arrive. We have guests who can't leave and a dire shortage of rooms.'

'I was raised in this country, Stefán, blizzards are not that big a deal,' Millie said, as her heart sank to her toes.

'As someone raised here, you should know how the weather influences travel, especially in winter, and you should know how important it is to stay well informed.'

Millie felt like an errant schoolgirl being repri-manded by the headmaster, but Stefán wasn't wrong. She *did* know better and she should've checked on what was happening with the weather. But when she got to the airport, her flight was on time and she'd assumed all was well.

'This one is going to be one of the worst in two

decades.' Stefán twisted his hands together. 'As per our email, we cancelled your reservation because you didn't confirm your arrival and we needed the room. We do not have a room for you.'

Dammit! Millie cursed.

'You said that you grew up here,' Stefán said, looking hopeful. 'I don't suppose you have anyone you can stay with?'

Yes, Benedikt. But also, no. She wasn't going to ask her husband/stranger whether she could ride out the storm with him. What if he had a lover living with him? Having his wife in the spare room would be, at best, problematic.

Aargh!

'I will try to find you accommodation, Ms Piper, but it might require you to share a room with another single female guest.'

Millie couldn't think of anything worse than having to be cooped up in a hotel room with a stranger. That sounded truly awful. 'I'll phone someone,' Millie told Stefán.

'Thank you,' Stefán replied. 'I will not start with my calls until I know whether or not you have been successful. I *do* hope you come right, Ms Piper.'

She did, too. She'd come to Iceland to ask her husband for a divorce, but now she'd have to ask Benedikt for help, too.

Blast!

She wouldn't get a place to stay, or a divorce, if she didn't call the man. Ignoring the nauseous feeling in her stomach, Millie did what she'd never had

cause to before and placed a video call to Benedikt.
He'd given Millie a mobile phone number the day
they married and this was the first time she'd used it.

'Millie, are you all right?'

She blinked at the sound of his chocolate-over-
gravel voice, which was deeper than most. His face
in her tiny screen came in focus and she took in
those still familiar features, that ruggedly angular
face, his high cheekbones and sensual mouth. His
eyes were a deep blue, tinged with violet, and she
noticed flecks of grey hair within his blond hair. The
creases at the edges of his eyes were deeper than before. Millie wondered where he'd picked up his tan
and could easily imagine him on a windsurfer or a
surfboard, sunlight and seawater on his broad shoulders and muscular arms.

Millie met his eyes. He looked older, hotter and
even more inscrutable than he did twelve years ago.
'Hello, Benedikt. I'm glad this number still works.'

He lifted one shoulder, covered in what she could
see was a very expensive designer shirt. The discreet
logo on the pocket was a dead giveaway. He wore a
perfectly knotted mint-green tie.

'Millie, again, are you all right?'

'I'm fine, why wouldn't I be?' she asked.

He released a sigh and sat back, his shoulders
dropping. 'Forgive me for thinking that, the first
time I get a phone call from my wife, something
might be wrong.'

Fair point. Millie pushed her long fringe off her

forehead and tucked it behind her ear. 'Sorry, I didn't think about that.'

She should tell him why she was calling, but she felt like an idiot. Benedikt would surely never ignore his emails and be caught out by an approaching blizzard. She decided to make small talk to build up her courage to ask him a favour. The first in twelve years...

'So, I'm going to be attending Star Shine's Gala Concert on the twenty-second. It'll take place at the Harpa Concert Hall.'

Every five years, the foundation her mum had established held a benefit concert to raise funds for the foundation and, as Jacqui's daughter, she was always invited to attend. She'd missed the last one due to flu and the one before that because she hadn't felt ready to return to Iceland. Bettina, her mum's best friend and the CEO of the foundation, would tolerate no excuses this year.

It was also the twenty-fifth anniversary of the establishment of the foundation and Bettina wanted Millie to do a tribute speech to her mum. The Gala Concert was one of the major social events of the decade and the idea of talking to the great and good of Europe made her quake in her boots.

'I thought I'd let you know,' Millie added, feeling like an idiot.

'The foundations' trustees will be glad to hear that,' Benedikt calmly replied. As one of the country's most celebrated business people, he would've been at the top of the list to receive an invitation to purchase a ticket to the much-anticipated Gala Concert. She knew he'd attended previous concerts and Millie wondered if he'd bring a partner to the event this time, although he hadn't before. Should she bring someone? But who? And why did she feel it was weird to take a date knowing her husband would be attending the same event?

He's not your husband, Millie, he's the man you made a deal with. Stop being naive...

The silence between them turned awkward and Millie cast about for something else to speak about. 'I was also wondering if you knew about a safety deposit box. I've had a letter to say it's come up for renewal, but I don't know anything about it,' Millie gabbled, trying to fill the silence between them.

Millie named the bank and Benedikt shook his head. 'I wasn't aware you had one.'

'Me neither, but it was opened around the time we married,' Millie explained.

His expression didn't change—he was so hard to read—but his eyes narrowed, just a fraction, and his left eyebrow raised a millimetre, maybe two. 'Not by me,' he stated.

Millie wrinkled her nose. 'I suppose Magnús must've opened it on my behalf. But I wonder what's in it?'

'It could be anything,' Benedikt said 'The only way to find out what's in it is to open it yourself. They won't allow anyone else to. So, you came back to Iceland to check a safety deposit box?' he asked, sounding sceptical.

Millie wished she'd made the trip for something so simple, but...*no.*

I need to start a new chapter of my life. I need to move on. I need to ask you for a divorce.

'Partly.'

'Isn't this a busy time for you with people buying jewellery for Christmas gifts?'

He wasn't wrong—a Millie Piper ring or pendant or bracelet made a perfect, but very pricey, Christmas gift. But her clients understood quality and artistry couldn't be rushed and they'd put in their orders months in advance to avoid disappointment.

'No, I'm done until the new year. Then I'll have to start working on an emerald and diamond choker for the wife of an American internet billionaire. He bought some emeralds when he was in Colombia—' She was rambling, dammit. Benedikt still made her feel off balance and gauche. Millie gave herself a mental slap. She wasn't eighteen any more, she was a grown woman with a successful business!

It didn't help that he was treating her as though they'd spoken yesterday, as though her out-of-the-ether call wasn't in any way a surprise. Millie wanted to punch through his impenetrable façade and shake him.

I'm your wife, she wanted to scream, but that urge quickly faded.

She wasn't, not really. Not in any way it counted. She was just a woman he'd married so that they could both get Magnús out of their lives. She'd been lucky Benedikt agreed to marry her because she'd been on a fast track to self-destruction. While she'd thought up the scheme for them to marry, Benedikt had helped her step off the tracks and out of the way of an incoming train.

But he wouldn't have helped her if there hadn't been anything in it for him and she understood that. But why hadn't he asked for a divorce before now? When she had turned twenty-five, he handed her the control of her trust but agreed, when she asked him, to act as her financial adviser.

For a year she'd tried to follow his directions— buy this stock, sell that one, liquidate this account, open that one—but she'd made mistakes, costly mistakes. When Ben offered to take back the management of her investment portfolio, north of fifty million pounds, and her trust, she'd handed it back to him with a huge sigh of relief. He wasn't scared of all those zeros, but they petrified her.

But why did he do that for her? Why did he never ask to buy her out of the company, the international empire he'd grown and built? Why did he never ask for a divorce? Why didn't he cut ties with her years ago?

It wasn't as though they were friends—before their marriage they'd been barely more than acquaintances. That didn't change after she became his wife.

'Now that we've danced around a bush or two, are you going to tell me why you really called?' Benedikt asked.

Right. *That.*

'I'm in a bit of a pickle.' His gaze sharpened, but

he didn't pepper her with questions, he simply lifted one thick eyebrow and waited. 'I'm actually in the city, I landed a little while ago.' She saw curiosity flick over his face and spoke before he could ask any questions. 'But I didn't read my email from the hotel and it turns out that there's an incoming blizzard and they are overbooked.'

'And you need a place to stay,' he blandly stated.

She pulled her bottom lip between her teeth. 'The manager said he would try to find me a room, but he looks as though he's about to have a panic attack. And I get the sense that, because I didn't read his don't-come-to-Iceland-because-a-blizzard-is-coming-and-you-didn't-confirm email, I'm way down on his list of priorities.'

'Why did you fly in now? The concert isn't for another two weeks. Why didn't you wait?' he asked.

That was a very good question. Maybe it was because, once she made up her mind, she needed to put her plan into action. Because if she didn't speak to him now, she might lose her nerve and not face him at all. Having a baby was her primary goal, but there were things she needed to do first. Getting a divorce was the first bullet point on her 'Steps to Falling Pregnant' list.

She couldn't explain any of that now, not in an increasingly crowded lobby and not over the phone. 'Can we talk about that when I see you? But, for now, can you suggest a place for me to stay?'

'I should be able to manage that.'

'At a hotel?' she asked, sounding hopeful.

'Mmm.'

Excellent. Staying wherever Benedikt stashed her would be a lot better than sharing a room with a stranger. Being one of the most influential business people in the country, Millie was pretty sure he would be able to find her a hotel room somewhere in the city. Hotel managers were always eager to do favours for someone who wielded as much power and financial clout as Benedikt did.

And, yes, a fancy room in an excellent hotel would cost her a lot of money, but she could afford it and she'd ride out the storm in comfort.

Millie released an audible sigh of relief and looked around the lobby to see Stefán looking at her. She gave him the thumbs up and he looked, momentarily, relieved. Then he turned back to talk to another guest and Millie knew he'd mentally crossed her off his to-do list and had moved on.

'Where are you?' Benedikt asked her.

Millie gave him the address of the hotel. 'Okay, stay put. I'll send my driver to pick you up. He'll know where to take you.'

Millie shook her head. 'That's not necessary, Benedikt, I can order a taxi.'

Benedikt just stared at her and Millie sighed. She should dig her heels and be a little more vociferous in her arguments but a) that stare was pretty damn intimidating and b) she knew he had numerous personal assistants to do his bidding. It wasn't as though he was going to personally run to her rescue—he'd send a minion to yank her out of her jam.

Millie nodded. 'Okay, thank you, I'll wait here for your driver. I appreciate your help. I'd also appreciate it if you could spare some time for us to meet. Obviously only when the blizzard is over and regular activities resume.'

'I'll be around,' Benedikt assured her. She saw a ghost of a smile touch his lips and his eyes lightened to the colour of a deep, dark sapphire. 'It'll be...*interesting* to see you again, Millie.'

She managed a small smile and disconnected the call. She was looking forward to seeing him. Madness, since she rarely thought of the man. He was still, as he'd always been, on the periphery of her life.

Her husband. Sort of.

CHAPTER TWO

DÉJÀ VU.

It felt like yesterday, but it had been twelve years since she last took this lift to Benedikt's office. She'd been eighteen years old and she'd been quaking in her boots. At nearly thirty, she wasn't quaking, but her stomach was definitely doing a number on her.

She looked at the tall man who'd followed her into the lift. When he walked into the hotel lobby earlier, he'd introduced himself as Einar Petersson, Benedikt's assistant. He had, he explained, instructions to take her to PR Reliance International Headquarters.

'Why did Benedikt ask you to bring me here?' Millie asked. Einar said he spoke little English, but Millie suspected he understood a lot more than he'd let on. She'd asked him the same question earlier and then, like now, he'd spread his hands out, looked blank and lifted his shoulders.

Oh, well, it wasn't as though she had somewhere else to go. She'd checked her weather app and the blizzard was supposed to start in a few hours. They were predicting very high winds—up to one hundred miles per hour in the north—and a massive snow dump, but the storm would only sweep in in a few hours. She had time to get to wherever Benedikt had arranged for her to go.

The lift doors opened and Einar guided her past an empty desk towards a long, wide office with floor-to-ceiling glass walls. She frowned and looked around. Extensive renovations had been done to the building. If she wasn't mistaken, the walls between Benedikt's office and the office Magnús had used had been knocked down to make a light and airy space with a huge desk and a seating area.

Einar opened the glass door and ushered her inside. He gestured for her to take a seat on one of the couches, but she crossed the room to the floor-to-ceiling windows. A wooden terrace ran the length of the room and lights flickered from a glass and steel building to the left. She recognised it as being the famous Harpa Concert Hall. It was a spectacular view at night, lights danced across the sea, but Millie knew Benedikt's office views would be equally spectacular in daylight.

Millie ran her fingers along the back of a sleek, Scandinavian-inspired couch. A massive flat-screen TV dominated another wall and there was a telescope in the corner, its nose pointing at the sky.

She wondered if Ben could see the Northern Lights from here. As a child, she remembered taking a trip with her mum north and they'd stayed in a cabin in the woods somewhere. They'd spent four nights sitting around a fire, bundled up in their all-weather gear, watching the sky flicker with ribbons of green and yellow light. She'd been entranced by the depth of colour and never forgot the experience.

Her mum had promised another trip, but time passed and, before they knew it, their time together was over. Millie was determined to see them again—spent a lot of time watching videos on YouTube—and she wanted to see the full light show instead of the trailer she'd witnessed as a kid.

Einar walked over to a trolley in the corner of the room and Millie saw it held coffee cups and a modern, silver, coffee jug. The smell of excellent coffee drifted over to her and she wondered where Benedikt was. Judging by all the empty offices she'd passed, all his staff had been sent home already.

As Einar walked over to her, carrying a cup of coffee, she placed a hand on her stomach, hoping to still the butterflies flapping their wings renting space in there. She was nervous about meeting Benedikt and she shouldn't be. He was nothing more than a man with whom she'd struck a deal a lifetime ago.

A marriage deal, but still a deal.

It was time to end it, to move on to the next chapter in her life. She'd have a family, even if it was one she had to make herself. She was so sick of living alone and rattling around her empty, quiet flat. She wanted a baby to love, someone who couldn't be taken from her. She wanted hugs and laughter, someone to cuddle, to fill up her empty apartment and break the long silences.

She wasn't a child any more, she was nearly thirty, for goodness sake! She'd done what she thought she should: she'd been to university, partied at Glastonbury and Burning Man, got her degree and established a career where she could make good money and set her own hours. She was financially secure and it was time to do something she'd been thinking about for years...

But as much as she wanted a child, as lonely as she was, she couldn't trust a man to share her life and family with. When you realised your mum, the person you thought loved you more than life itself, had lied to you and kept you in the dark, it made trusting anyone else impossible.

That, and she'd witnessed Magnús's possessive streak. He'd wanted her mum all to himself, all the time. He hated Jacq's independent streak and resented Millie being in her mum's life. Magnús's love was tainted by a slick, destructive layer of control, sprinkled with obsession.

She'd never let that happen to her and wasn't prepared to take the chance on loving someone who might end up trying to change or cage her. She didn't want her baby to have to live with, or witness, anything similar.

Millie heard the sound of a throat clearing, blinked and looked at the coffee cup Einar held out to her. She took it with a shaking hand and immediately lifted the cup to her lips, desperate for a jolt of the hot liquid, for a hit of caffeine. Being back in

Iceland, the first time in for ever, had her feeling more emotional and off balance than she'd expected.

She had to pull herself together before she met Benedikt.

'Hello, Millie.'

Millie spun around, saw his tall frame standing at the door and tried to replace the cup on its saucer. She missed by a mile and coffee spilt on to the pale, hardwood floors and splattered over her boots.

Damn. She'd really been looking forward to that cup of coffee.

As his assistant wiped up coffee, Ben looked at Millie, taking in her similarities, cataloguing the differences. The black, Goth-inspired hair was gone and so was the thick makeup she wore back then. She'd pulled her hair, as sleek as an otter's coat and roughly the same colour, into a sleek tail and her makeup, if she wore any, was understated. Dark eyelashes and gently arched eyebrows framed her clear, light green eyes. Once too skinny, she'd filled out and his mouth watered as he took in her gentle curves. Put simply, she was gorgeous.

'Hi, Benedikt,' she murmured, her hand on her throat.

The last person he'd expected to see today, or see any time soon, was Millie. He'd been preparing to leave his office when her call came in—he'd already sent everyone but Einar home. That she was in his city shocked him and he was insanely curious as to why she wanted to meet.

She'd never expressed any interest in the company and he made all the decisions concerning their now jointly owned business. They communicated via infrequent emails.

They'd been legally married for more than a decade, but he knew little about her and her life.

So why was she here?

Ben forced his feet to move and hoped his normal implacable mask was in place as he walked over to her. He took her elegant hand in his, felt the tingle of attraction skitter over his hand and up his arm, and bent his head to kiss her cheek. She smelled of wildflowers and something deeper, darker, sexier.

'Hello, M…'

Hell! Her name wouldn't move over his tongue. Shock held him rigid and his grip on her hand tightened. Was he about to stutter? *Now?* And after so long? It had been years since he'd struggled with his speech, but this woman—his *wife*—had his words catching in his throat.

He tried to stop the slide into the past, to push away the unrelenting memories of being a child, cursed with shyness and a terrible stutter, raised to believe he was a disappointment, frequently told his profound stutter was something he could overcome if he worked hard enough and wasn't ineffective and weak. His uninterested, nuclear engineer mother also thought mocking and denigrating him for his affliction would cure him of it sooner.

It hadn't.

He'd eventually, with no help from her, learned

how to converse normally. He thought he had his stutter under complete control until a year before Jacq's death. While trying to make a toast to his then bride-to-be at his engagement party, it had roared back into his life. His fiancé hadn't been impressed when he walked away from the podium after two sentences and ripped into him for not telling her he had a 'disability'.

That he'd met her at a business conference where he was the keynote speaker and hadn't stuttered once during his ninety-minute presentation, or since that day, went straight over her head. Accepting that his stutter only appeared when he felt emotional, he quickly found the solution: if he avoided emotion, his stutter would never raise its ugly head again. So far, his theory had proven true.

He and Millie weren't emotionally connected, so why did he stumble?

Recalling his training, and those hard, endless lessons, he took a deep breath and kissed Millie's other cheek to buy himself some time. He cleared his throat to gain another few moments of calm before he spoke. 'Hello, Millie. You're looking—'

Her eyebrows lifted. 'Older?'

He wanted to tell her she looked fantastic, that he hadn't expected her to pack such a punch. He settled for telling her she looked lovely. The girl he remembered had amused him and he'd admired her courage, but this woman had his knees melting and his heart thumping. He'd always mocked the idea of having butterflies in his stomach—it was such a

asinine notion!—but his were about to take flight.
Ben felt sweat pooling at the base of his spine and he
swallowed as his eyes drifted over her body, taking
in her full breasts, long legs and round hips.

His wife packed a hell of a sexual punch.

Ben stepped back and looked at Einar, who'd
crossed to the other side of his office to give them
some privacy. 'Would you please pour Ms Piper another coffee, Einar? Then you can go home.'

Einar nodded. 'Certainly.'

Einar did as he asked and, after reminding him
that the weather was closing in and he shouldn't daw-
dle, left him and Millie alone.

Ben checked his watch. He had to leave the office within the hour, no longer. That would give him
enough time to get home before conditions drasti-
cally deteriorated. Ben walked to the drinks trolley in the far corner of the room to pour himself a
whisky, which he threw back. He lifted the bottle
and nodded his approval. The whisky was part of a
limited run from a distillery in Speyside. Fantasti-
cally expensive, but exceptional. It was technically
too early to drink, but it wasn't every day his wife in
name only made an unexpected appearance.

'May I have one of those?'

He nodded, poured a decent measure into her
glass and carried the glass over to her. He pushed the
heavy tumbler into her hand and his fingers brushed
hers, a touch as light as a feather and as hot and
fast as an electrical shock. Power ran up his hand,
through his arm, and smacked into his heart. His

gaze connected with hers and found cool green lightning in her eyes. Her chin lifted, just a little, and he noticed the flush on her cheeks, the tick in her jaw.

He was old enough, experienced enough, to recognise their mutual attraction and the urge to drop his head was overwhelming.

Her scent swirled around him and he lowered his head just a fraction, the distance between their lips lessening. The air between them tasted of coffee and whisky. He was about to kiss Millie...

He was...

About to...

Kiss Millie.

The thought landed, his eyes flew open and he jerked up, stepped back and rubbed the back of his neck, utterly disconcerted at their instant, intense attraction.

This was Millie. His *wife*.

He pulled away, took a step back and pushed an agitated hand through his hair. Needing time, he picked up his phone, pretended to check for messages and tried to regulate his over-excited heart. Stupid thing. Its job was to pump blood, nothing else.

'I like the changes you made to your office,' Millie stated, after sitting on his couch and crossing one long leg over the other.

Thank God for the change of subject.

'When I bought the building, I refurbished the entire place,' Ben replied, keeping his eyes on his phone, needing a little time to take her in. She was everything, and more than, he'd thought she'd be.

The wild child was gone, and she'd come a long way in twelve years.

He knew a little about her…she'd attained a degree in art history, was a jewellery designer and owned and lived in an apartment in Notting Hill. He sent her company statements, which she never queried, and he paid her share of the profits into a bank account she provided. They weren't emotionally connected and there was never anything more between them than a piece of paper and a legal agreement.

She'd married him to avoid a jail sentence and take control of her life, he'd married her to take control of the business he loved, and they both got Magnús out of their lives permanently.

Ben sipped his whisky and felt the welcome burn in his throat. Millie drank hers and looked out the window, seemingly entranced by the view. He eyed her profile—which was lovely—and looked for something to say. *How was your flight?* seemed trite, *Welcome to Reykjavik* even more so.

He sighed. In a work environment, talking was never an issue and he was suave enough, unemotional enough, to talk a woman into bed. But when someone meant something to him—and as his wife and business partner and as Jacqui's daughter, Millie did, just a little—he found making small talk difficult. Keeping tabs on his stutter harder.

That she'd morphed from a girl who'd worn nothing but black as a teenager into one of the most beautiful, self-possessed, and stylish women he'd encountered in a long time didn't help at all. If she was just another woman he wanted, his words wouldn't stick in his throat. But she wasn't. And wanting Millie in all the ways he shouldn't rocked him to his core.

For the first ten years of his life, he could barely hold a conversation, and when he found someone with the patience to listen to what he had to say, they were both exhausted at the end of their discourse. Picking out words between the stutters was hard work for everyone. It was easier not to talk at all; if he kept silent then he didn't receive as many pitying glances and rolled eyes.

Memories, unbidden and unwelcome, rolled over him. At thirteen and already struggling to fit in at his local school, his mother, who wholly believed in the 'if you put your mind to it, you can achieve it' school of thought, decided that boarding school would *sort him out*.

If he thought he'd been bullied and teased before, it was nothing to what he endured at one of the best boys' schools in the country. If he tried to speak, he was bullied. If he didn't, he was bullied even more. He was the ultimate easy target and his frantic text messages and emails to his mum—he was far too upset to try to get the words out on a call—begging her to pull him out of school went unheeded. Four months into what, for him, was hell on earth, he knew nobody was riding in to save him and he was on his own.

He'd been on the point of running away when his English teacher stepped in and roped in the school's counsellor. She referred him to a speech therapist, who helped him get the worst of his stuttering under control. Then he signed up for a university trial, working with a language professor. Using his innovative techniques, Ben's stutter all but disappeared. The bullying died down when his stuttering did and his sudden growth spurt at fifteen also helped. Running and skiing made him fast and strong and he was able to fight back, which made him less of a target. He finally made friends and then girls also started paying him attention.

He learned, quite quickly, that females really did go for the strong and silent type.

As he got older, grew stronger, and more confident, his mother's once-powerful intellect started to diminish. As he gained knowledge, at school and university, his mum lost hers and the once sharp, cutting and undeniably charismatic woman grew confused, a victim of early-onset Alzheimer's. Her condition deteriorated rapidly and, in his last year of university, Ben made the hard decision to put his mother into a residential home. She'd screamed, insulted him and called him a million names. As her brain withered, she lost all her filters and informed him he should've had the abortion, she'd never wanted him, and that embarrassing stutter of his was a constant source of humiliation.

Six months later she passed away, the day after he graduated from university.

Wanting to get out of London, he'd applied for a job at PR Reliance in Reykjavik and was pulled under Jacqui's wing. He not only found her knowl-edgeable, and easy to talk to, but in her he found the older sister and best friend he'd so desperately needed.

She'd been the only person he talked to about his struggles to communicate and, with her encourage-ment, he started dating, had a few relationships and then fell in love. When Margrét tore into him at their engagement party, yelling at him for embarrassing her in front of her family and friends, it was Jacqui who'd steered him out of the room.

Jacqui didn't agree with his decision to avoid love and relationships, she believed being emotional re-quired mental strength and bravery. Ben didn't often disagree with Jacqui, but he did about that. Emotion was a weakness and one he wouldn't tolerate.

It was highly problematic that Jacqui's daughter made his words—temporarily, he hoped—stick in his throat.

And that wasn't, in any way, acceptable. Theirs was a legal arrangement, nothing more or less. Busi-ness.

Get it together, Jónsson.

He sat on the chair opposite the couch, leaned back, hitched his suit pants up and placed his ankle on his opposite knee. Ben wanted to see her in a busi-ness light, but the impulse to push the coffee table out of the way, pull her band from her hair and lower his mouth and body to hers was unbelievably strong.

He wanted to know how she tasted, whether the skin where her neck and jaw met was as soft as it looked. He wanted her hands sliding down his stomach, over his hip, her lips on his jaw, his neck, his hipbone…*lower*. He wanted to pull her jersey up her body and cover her full breast with his hands, trace her curves, kiss her hip, her lower back, between her legs…

He *wanted* her. With a ferocity that rocked him. Women were great, he liked them—they were smart and creative and intuitive—and he enjoyed them in bed and out. But he had never felt the overwhelming need to discover, to explore, as he did with Millie.

Annoyed with himself, Ben took a deep breath and forced himself to think about business. Why was she affecting him like this? What was it about her that made him question his control over his tongue? Women didn't do this to him, he didn't *allow* it.

'So, why are you in Reykjavik, Millie? On the phone you said you needed to talk…what about?'

Ben noticed the tension in her neck and how her spine straightened. A knot formed in his stomach and he knew, without her needing to say anything, what she was about to say.

He'd been expecting this conversation for years. 'You want a divorce, don't you?' he stated.

Her eyes slammed into his. 'How did you know?'

'It wasn't hard to work out, Millie. You've never asked for a face-to-face meeting before, we always correspond via email. There is only one thing you could want from me that would require a face-to-face meeting and that's a request to end our marriage.'

She nodded before slowly placing her glass on the

coffee table. He noticed her trembling fingers. 'It's been a long time, Ben, and I think it's time.'

'I'm perfectly happy with the way things are,' he told her.

'Don't you want...' she hesitated '...more?'

'More what?'

'More than a convenient marriage! What about being in a loving relationship, having kids, establishing a family?'

He had no intention of doing any of the above. He linked his hands across his stomach and wished they were on her. 'I've never wanted to get married—'

Okay, that was a lie, he had wanted to once, but he'd learned the hard way that the people you loved could hurt you the most. He wouldn't love again. It was very simple.

'I have affairs, but I don't get involved. I have never had the desire to put a ring on anybody else's finger.'

Not quite a lie, but not quite the truth either.

A marriage of convenience to Millie suited him perfectly. They hadn't put any restrictions on what they could do or who they could be with. They were both free to take lovers and had done so. They didn't report to each other or even kept each other updated. So the only reason Millie could want a divorce after so long was that she wanted more than what she had right now. A proper, committed relationship, perhaps even a proper marriage.

Could he blame her for that? Of course not, she deserved to be loved, deserved to have a man adore her. He couldn't be that man for her, not now and not ever. He could never be that man for anyone. And he would never risk getting so close to a person again— being emotionally sliced and diced by his mum, then his fiancé, was more than enough.

He tried to smile, but found it incredibly hard. When he spoke, he didn't achieve the lightness he was aiming for. 'So who's the lucky guy?' he asked.

Millie looked at him, her eyebrows pulling down. 'What?'

At the thought of another man kissing her, wrapping his arms around her slight body, doing all the things he wanted to do, Ben's gut twisted. The whisky he'd swallowed sloshed in his stomach and he felt seasick.

Nobody affected him like this.

It had to be the shock of seeing Millie all grown up, her now being a woman and not a girl. That's *all* it could be. All he'd allow it to be. Anything else was impossible. Yes, maybe he was attracted to her, she was lovely—who wouldn't be?—but he was old enough to know he didn't need to act on it. In fact, it would be far more sensible not to. Less complicated. Smarter.

'I'm not seeing anyone, Ben,' Millie told him.

He frowned and her words sank into his jittery brain. 'Then what's the problem? Why do you want things to change?'

Millie stood and walked over to the glass doors that led on to the balcony and watched fat snowflakes fall out of the sky. They were running out of time, the blizzard was roaring in, but he stayed where he was and watched her.

Millie placed her forehead against the cool glass, her shoulders rose and fell and she released a long sigh. Her breath put condensation on the window and she dragged a finger through the wet patch. When she turned, he saw the frustration in her eyes and the tilt of her chin implied she could be stubborn. Like mother, like daughter.

You don't get apples from orange trees, Jónsson.

She managed a self-deprecating smile: 'Aren't you sick of me? Aren't I a millstone around your neck? I'm happy to sell you my stake in the company. I'm a grown woman and I could find someone else to act as the trust's financial adviser.'

'I don't have the money to buy out your stake right now, not without finding investors and taking out loans with crippling interest rates, and it's not top of my list of priorities. And you've been able to look after everything for many years now, Millie, and I've never doubted your ability to do so. You could manage your own money—'

'But then I'd have to learn about the stock market, amortisation, capital gains and the difference between a hedge fund and a mutual fund.' She shuddered. 'I don't understand any of it.'

'You don't want to understand because it bores you.'

'It really does. You're so much better at investments and things. And you said you didn't mind,' she muttered.

'I don't mind,' he pointed out. 'It takes me minimal time and it's something I'm still happy to do.'

Her trust was incredibly healthy, partly because he made the same sound decisions for her as he did for himself, but mostly because she seldom pulled money from its overflowing coffers. She'd only taken money to buy her Notting Hill apartment and her car, purchases he'd approved of. She didn't need his approval, but he admired her willingness to support herself and establish a career without using her inheritance as a cushion.

Being a workaholic himself, he appreciated hard work.

Ben climbed to his feet and went to stand beside her. He pushed his shoulder into the glass and looked down at her bent head. 'If you want a divorce, Millie, that's fine. It's not as though our arrangement was supposed to last for ever. And I would be happy to stay on as your financial adviser if that's what you wanted me to do.'

Her gorgeous green eyes, the colour of green grapes, met his. 'You would?'

'Sure.'

He wanted to touch her, to stroke his thumb over her lower lip, across her cheekbone, down the cords of her lovely, long neck. He jammed his hands into his suit pants to stop himself from doing something so idiotic.

'I just want to know *why*, Millie,' he said. He wasn't good with unanswered questions.

She managed a smile, just a small one. 'My mum

always said that you were tenacious and that you never gave up. I guess that's how you expanded the business so quickly and came to be one of Europe's best business people.'

'So what's the real reason you want a divorce, Millie?'

She sighed before looking him in the eye. 'I want a baby. And I didn't think it's fair to have one while still being married to you.'

CHAPTER THREE

MILLIE HELD HER breath while Benedikt processed her words. While he did have an inscrutable face, his eyes were a different story. A lighter blue meant he was amused, darker meant he was either angry or turned on and lightning-tinged purple indicated he was shocked. And, yes, a lightning storm was happening in his eyes right now.

'You want a baby?' he asked, his voice holding the slightest hint of a croak.

'I'm not getting any younger, Benedikt,' she told him. But more than that, she was very tired of being on her own, of having no one to love. And loving a baby was the safest option she could think of.

'You are a few months off your thirtieth birthday, you're not about to qualify for an old person's pension,' he snapped. 'I'm thirty-eight! What's your age got to do with any of this?'

'Apparently, eighteen is the best time, physiologically, for a woman to have a child. And, from her mid-thirties, a woman is thought to be a geriatric mother.'

'That's ridiculous,' he snapped.

'That's science,' she retorted. She lifted her hand, her palm facing him. 'We're getting off track... I've always wanted a baby and I think it's the right time to have one. My business is established, I work from home and I make my own hours. I can afford to hire help and, most importantly, I think I'm mentally ready to invite a little human into my life.'

Sometimes her dreams about holding her baby felt so real, she could smell his sweet smell, hear his cry and feel his warm little body snuggled into her arm. Millie felt the familiar tug in her womb and nodded. Yes, she wanted her little boy...

Benedikt rubbed the back of his neck before pulling down the knot of his tie. He opened the top button to his shirt and pulled the tie over his head, still knotted, and jammed it into the inside pocket of his suit jacket, which he then yanked off and tossed over the back of the couch.

Millie watched as he rolled up the sleeves of his shirt, marvelling at strong forearms covered in blond hair. When he was done, he rolled his shoulders and tipped his head up to look at the ceiling.

'So you want a child.'

'I do,' Millie told him. 'But I don't think I should be married when I have one.'

Benedikt sat on the back of the low couch and stretched out his long legs. 'You told me that you don't have a partner, so how are you going to "have" one, Millie?'

She sent an anxious glance towards his window

and grimaced. 'Shouldn't we be going? There's a storm coming,' she reminded him.

He glanced at his limited edition Patek Philippe watch. 'We still have some time before we need to leave. I don't live that far away and it will only take me twenty minutes, even in this weather, to get home.'

'Yes, but you have to drop me off first,' Millie told him. When he didn't say anything, she narrowed her eyes. Oh, no. *No, no, no.*

'I'm not staying with you, Jónsson,' she told him. *Uh-uh, no way.*

'Einar made some calls and he couldn't get you a hotel room at such late notice. And it made no sense to keep calling when I have a perfectly good guest suite.'

A guest suite was fine for one night, but not if they were housebound because of the weather!

'It's a big house, Millie,' Ben told her. 'It has a gym and sauna and a library. We won't be tripping over each other.'

'We don't know each other!' Millie wailed. She didn't want to spend a couple of days cooped up with a man to whom she was intensely attracted.

'We're married,' Ben calmly pointed out.

Back then he was an adult and she'd been a young woman, looking to spread her wings and leave the city. They had been miles apart, mentally and socially. Twelve years later, the gap between them had narrowed substantially. He was hot and sexy and she hadn't been this attracted to a man in years. If ever.

She'd wanted him to kiss her earlier. Had been about to lift on to her toes to meet his mouth when he'd pulled back. Disappointment and frustration rolled over her, hot and sour. Honestly, had she left her brain and self-control back in London? And how was she supposed to share a house with a man she desperately wanted to see naked? Nope, not happening. She needed a hotel room, a room in an Airbnb, a stable or a caravan. Anything.

'I can't—'

'You'll have to because there's nowhere else for you to go,' Ben crisply told her and she knew she'd lost the argument. She had to be sensible and take whatever accommodation was on offer. She was out of choices.

'Let's get back to *how* you plan on getting pregnant.'

Why was he hung up on that? Why was that an issue and why did it concern him? But she wasn't ashamed of wanting a family, nor was she ashamed of her plan of how to fall pregnant. She wanted a family, she was so sick of being alone. 'I'm going to choose a sperm donor and be artificially inseminated, Benedikt.'

He pulled a face and Millie threw up her hands. 'Well, what other choice do I have? To go pub or club trawling at the right time of the month, find a guy I like the look of and have a one-night stand, crossing my fingers that he isn't a psycho?'

'That wouldn't be wise,' Benedikt stated.

'Of course not,' Millie retorted, unsure of why

she was discussing this with him. They might be married, but they *weren't* friends. 'That's why I'm going to choose what I hope will be a nice man from a website that gives me statistics about his medical history and IQ and looks and genes. And pray he's a decent human being!'

Benedikt's eyes clashed with hers and Millie wondered what he was thinking, trying to ignore what *she* was thinking: he would make the most delicious father himself. He was tall, athletic, smart as a whip and not a psycho. He was just a hardworking, driven billionaire currently married to her. There was no way he'd consider…

You're being ridiculous, Millie! You're asking for a divorce so that you can cut the strings with this man, and asking him to give you his biological matter would be like using a ship's rope to bind you together.

She was just being fanciful, feeling a little disconcerted and off balance about being back in Reykjavik—the place held so many good and bad memories. Memories of her lovely mum and her awful dad…*stepdad*.

Meeting Benedikt again…

Flip, how she wished he'd grown plump and started to go bald, was in a relationship himself or was too busy to see her. If she'd managed to avoid him, then she wouldn't be feeling all hot and bothered, tingly and weird. Yes, Benedikt made her feel shaky and off her game.

'So, what's the next step?' she asked, placing her open palms on the glass behind her back.

'I drive you back to my place and settle you into my guest suite.'

'I meant with us getting a divorce, Benedikt. Shall we see a lawyer together, get our own? I'm not going to claim anything from you...' She couldn't—they'd signed a prenup and their individual assets were protected. Their divorce should be a quick and easy process.

Benedikt looked, surprisingly, a little disconcerted. He always seemed so together, so unshockable—he'd barely blinked at her offer of marriage—and she hadn't thought he could be caught off guard. 'Uh... I... I'm not sure. I need to look into it.'

He paused, hauled in some air and paused again. He was a confident and super-capable businessman, maybe he had a thing about picking and choosing the right words. 'I can set up a meeting with my lawyer and he can advise us on how to go forward,' he stated. 'He's also my cousin and closest friend. Olivier is one of the best lawyers in the country.'

Of course he was—a man in Benedikt's position wouldn't have anyone but the best. 'Could we meet tomorrow?' Millie asked. 'I fly tomorrow afternoon.' Then she remembered the storm. 'I *was* flying tomorrow afternoon.'

'I'll contact Olivier now,' he said. Benedikt picked up his phone and typed in a super-fast message.

'Olivier is working from home and he's suggested a video call. We can talk about legalities when we get

back to my place. He's annoyed because he wanted
to meet you in person.'

'Why?' Millie asked, confused.

'Because he's been your trust's lawyer for over
eight years, Millie.'

Oh, right. *Olafson*. She'd seen correspondence
from his law offices many times over the years. He'd
answered many of her legal questions and she wanted
to meet him, too. 'Maybe we could all have lunch
when I come back on the twenty-second.'

'I'm not going to be in the country, I'm flying
to St Barth's that day for an old friend's stag weekend,' Benedikt told her. Oh. Well, that answered the
question about whether he'd be attending the gala
concert or not.

'We'll video call him when we get home,' Benedikt said, standing up. 'We do need to get going, I do
not want to be driving when the storm hits.'

She was going home with him and they would
be alone.

Millie picked up her bag, feeling tired, out of her
depth and emotionally drained. She looked around.
'I don't know where my luggage is, Benedikt,' she
told him.

'For goodness sake, call me Ben,' he told her, ges-
turing for her to leave his office in front of him. He
flipped off some light switches. 'And Einar trans-
ferred your luggage to my car.'

Millie followed Ben to the lifts and stepped into
one that was empty. In the confined space, she in-
haled Ben's cologne, a fresh scent that made her want

to bury her nose in his throat, and lick her way across his collarbone.

Once more she was bombarded with thoughts of how Ben would look naked, whether that sensual mouth delivered wicked kisses and what it would feel like to have his broad, masculine hands moving over her skin. She hadn't felt this attracted to a man in…ages. Truthfully, she'd never felt this much this quickly. Nobody ever had her mentally undressing him, thinking about his mouth and his hands…

She wanted him and she *so* didn't want to want her husband. And she could never, ever let him suspect she was attracted to him.

This marriage of convenience was now very inconvenient indeed!

Ben's car was a four-wheel drive Range Rover with all the bells, whistles and, best of all, heated seats. The wind had picked up and it was snowing quite hard but, because she knew Ben had been driving in extreme conditions for twenty-plus years, Millie settled back in her seat.

As they drove through Reykjavik she noticed the exquisite shops, decorated for Christmas, and an abundance of white fairy lights. She had hoped to take a tour of Reykjavik to see the city decorated with its Christmas lights, but she didn't know if she'd manage it this trip. Twelve years ago, she'd felt like a local, now she was a little better than a tourist.

Millie looked at Ben behind the wheel and took in his strong profile. He'd draped his wrist over the steering wheel and she'd felt a buzz of lust between her legs. She'd been in Iceland for just a few hours and spent a lot of that time thinking about his hands and how they would feel on her bare skin.

She'd spent almost as much time imagining his mouth, how he would taste…how amazing he would look naked. He had an athlete's build, tall, rangy and muscled, and she suspected that a few of his muscles had muscles of their own.

They stopped at a traffic light and Ben reached across her legs to open the glove compartment, his hand brushing her knee and her thigh. He murmured a quick apology as he pulled out a phone charger, the side of his hand skimming over the top of her hand.

He plugged his charger in and Millie noticed a muscle ticking in the side of his jaw. The atmosphere in the car turned heavy and sultry, wickedly intense. He looked at her and they exchanged another of those I-can't-believe-how-much-I-want-you glances.

Then the traffic light changed to green, Ben hit the button to let in a gust of fresh, snow-tinged air and the moment passed. It was, she supposed, a viable alternative to a cold shower.

Her unexpected attraction to him was both tiresome and problematic. Millie wiggled in her seat and slipped out of her coat. She'd never before thought of Ben in terms of sex or being stripped of his clothes. Up until yesterday, he'd been the name at the end of infrequent email messages.

Most days, and for most of their marriage, she rarely thought of him and she never, not once, found her marriage to him any sort of handbrake. The terms of their engagement were clear: it was a business deal and their lives were never, in any way, to be impacted by it. They both had the freedom to see other people, sleep with other people, and do what they wanted when they wanted.

She had no idea how many lovers Ben had had—she'd seen the occasional picture of him with some socialite or celebrity at fancy functions over the years—but she knew he'd been anything but a monk. Neither had she been a nun. She'd had two relationships at university, neither of which panned out—she wouldn't let them—and another two lovers since then.

The thing was, while she could never see herself getting married and settling down—if she couldn't trust her mum, the person she loved the most and whom she always believed loved her, to tell her the truth about her biological father, how could she trust anyone? Ever? And love and trust went hand in hand. Neither was she cut out for casual sex and random affairs. They were fine for a lot of women, but sharing her body was an intimate act and sex with a stranger made her feel a little ick.

So she was stuck in no man's land. Because she didn't like hurting guys and didn't like to lead them on, she always laid her cards on the table. If she liked a guy enough after a couple of months of dating, she made it clear she wasn't interested in a long-term relationship. Some stuck around, mostly because they thought they could change her mind, but most didn't.

She kept a close eye on the ones who stayed. If she thought their feelings for her were deepening, she called it quits.

But she'd never had such an intense reaction to a man, ever. Something about Benedikt called to her and she was both mentally and physically curious. She wanted to know why he'd stayed married to her for so long, why he was so anti settling down, why he was such a lone wolf. She wanted to know his likes and dislikes, what made him laugh, and the things that caused him to feel mad, sad and frustrated. But most of all, she wanted to know how good he was in bed.

She thought he'd be excellent, even brilliant. Possibly, *probably*, mind-blowing.

Millie looked out the window and told herself to get a grip. She was in the country for, at most, the next thirty-six to forty-eight hours and nothing could, or would, happen. They'd get divorced, pretty quickly because they'd been separated for ever and because it was something they both wanted. They weren't going to fight over assets or money or kids and, in a couple of months, she'd be free of her husband on paper, the man she married but didn't know.

In January, she'd make a concerted effort to wrap her head around a sperm donor. She'd find somebody nice, smart and, hopefully, sexy. And in a year or two, she'd go back to the same donor to try for a sibling for her toddler. She'd been an only child and hated it, and desperately wished she had someone who knew her and her backstory, someone to whom she could talk about her parents and the past.

Millie crossed her legs as they passed through a pretty neighbourhood with old houses. 'Where do you live?' she asked Ben.

He looked at her quickly before returning his eyes to the road. 'Ah, I inherited my father's house close to Ingólfur Square.'

Her mum and his dad had been friends and Millie vaguely remembered Jon's house. It was, if her memory was right, built of grey stone and Jon always boasted that it was one of the older houses in the city. 'I remember the hallway had lots of wood,' she told him.

'That's the one. I did quite a bit of remodelling. The wooden panelling is gone, but I kept the original parquet flooring and renovated the kitchen and bathrooms,' he explained.

She really hoped he left the garden alone. She'd built fairy houses in the small backyard and imagined that butterflies perched on the rims of the moss-covered urns.

'At some point, I have to do something about the garden, but it's been way down on my list of priorities,' Benedikt explained.

'Do not touch the garden,' she told him, sounding fierce. For some reason, she could see her little boy climbing the thick branches of the tree near the wooden gate, looking for Huldufólk, the country's version of elves. She imagined a little girl building and decorating a house from sticks and stones on the stone flags so one of the hidden folk families could make it their home.

She saw his eyebrows shoot up and waved her hand away. She was projecting her desire for children on to him and felt heat in her cheeks. 'Sorry, it's your garden and you can do what you want with it. I loved it, though. I thought it was magical.'

'Are you sure you are remembering the right place?' he joked. 'The one with the cracked flagstones and the slippery moss paths?'

'That's the one. I don't ever remember seeing you there.'

'I only visited my dad a few times when I was a kid.'

Millie half turned to face him. 'Did you ever come to our house?'

He tapped his finger on the steering wheel. 'Once, twice maybe. Magnús didn't like your mum bringing work home. And he and I didn't get along.'

'Join the club,' Millie muttered.

'I do remember a barn and Jacqui telling me about her animals.'

'Mum and I were both crazy about animals,' Millie replied, smiling. 'If anything was sick, pretty much anywhere within fifty kilometres, it ended up in our barn. It drove Magnús mad.'

The animals took up Jacqui's attention, just like Millie and her business did, something Magnús hated. He'd wanted her mum all to himself, all the time. No wonder she was terrified of being controlled.

'Magnús frequently threatened to have the animals put down. I spent so many nights wide awake, worried that the rabbit or horse or pig we'd just rescued wouldn't be there in the morning.'

Benedikt's expression darkened. 'Really? Man, he was an unfeeling sod.'

That wasn't the worst of it. 'The week after Mum died, that's exactly what happened. I came home from school and all the animals in the barn had been removed. He told me they'd been relocated, but he wouldn't tell me where they were. I'm convinced he had them put down.'

Those animals had been a distraction from her grief, a connection to her mum, and Magnús had ripped them away from her, she explained to Ben. She wasn't sure why she was telling him this, maybe it was because he knew, and didn't like, Magnús. Because he understood the reasons behind her hatred for her stepfather.

Ben's jaw tightened and she knew he was angry for her. So was she. She was so angry for the vulnerable girl she'd been.

'What else did he do?' he asked. 'I know there was more.'

He was right. Magnús hadn't had a sliver of sympathy for her in the weeks and months after her mum's death. It had been such a desolate, lonely, awful time. 'Oh, he wouldn't let me have any input into her funeral and he insisted on white lilies at the funeral when he knew her favourite flowers were gerbera daisies.

'Soon after the animals left, I came home to find

strangers packing up my mum's clothes,' she said. 'I called him and screamed at him, told him that there were things of hers I wanted, that he had no right to ask strangers to pack up her belongings.'

'He told me not to be hysterical, she was gone and the sooner I got used to the idea, the easier it would be for him. I was becoming tiresome, he told me, and he was sick of seeing my long face day in and day out.'

'And this was how many weeks after she died?' Ben asked, horrified.

'Two? Maybe three?'

'What a complete moron,' Ben stated. 'I never suspected any of this, Millie.'

'Why would you? You were a part of Mum's working life,' she replied. She played with the hem of her jersey, knowing she could be more candid with Ben than she could be with anyone else. He had known her mum well.

'To the world, my mum was this independent, incredibly strong woman, but nobody knew how much Magnús tried to control her. He hated anything that took her time away from him and resented the attention Mum gave me. If you weren't fully focused on Magnús, he thought you were ignoring him.'

'I only knew him in a business environment, but he could be a difficult bastard.'

Whenever Millie thought she might be missing out on something by not having a man in her life, she remembered what her mum went through with Magnús. She'd never allow that to happen to her.

She'd rather be single and uncontrolled than married and miserable.

'So after your mum died, you thought that rebelling was a good idea,' Ben murmured. Millie stiffened and then realised there was no judgement in his voice.

'I was hurt, angry and confused. I wanted his attention so I acted up. After I found out he wasn't my dad, I wanted to punish him for not loving me and for not telling me sooner he wasn't my real dad, for *not* being my real dad,' she explained, her shoulders up around her ears. 'I tried to make his life as difficult as possible.'

Ben mused, 'I was, reluctantly, impressed by how well you handled his Ferrari. You were clocked at some ridiculous speed on the highway. How did you manage not to kill yourself in that thing?'

She grinned, remembering the exhilaration of having all that power under her control. 'I was, am, a very good driver,' she told him. 'I did clip a pavement going too fast turning into a one-way street. I put a deep gouge in his midnight-blue paintwork.'

'Good for you,' Ben told her. He flipped the windscreen wipers on to a higher setting and Millie noticed that snow was falling in a steady stream. While she'd been nattering away, the weather had turned worse.

'Are we close to your house?' she asked.

'Very,' Ben assured her. 'We'll get home safely, I promise.'

He pushed a button on his steering wheel and

tuned into a local radio station. The female presenter was talking in fast Icelandic and Millie quickly lost track of her words. Her Icelandic was very rusty indeed.

She caught Ben's grimace. 'It's getting worse,' he said. 'The northern parts of the country are being hammered. The city will be shut down tomorrow. It'll remain shut for a day, maybe two.'

It took Millie a moment to process the information. 'So, my flight tomorrow afternoon will be cancelled?'

He nodded. 'Definitely.'

She grimaced. 'I have an appointment with the bank tomorrow, to get into my safety deposit box.'

'They will postpone it,' Ben told her, swinging into a snow-covered drive. He pushed a button on his visor and a double garage door rolled up. He entered the tidy garage, filled with big boy toys, and parked his SUV next to a Ducati superbike. A snowmobile and a jet ski sat on trailers. 'If you need to get back to London urgently, then you should try to rebook your flight as soon as possible, maybe go on standby to get the first flight out.'

Millie shook her head. 'I'm not in that much of a hurry. There's nothing I *need* to get back for, I'm free until the New Year. But I don't want to take advantage of your hospitality,' she added when he didn't reply. She rooted around in her bag and pulled out her phone. 'Can you give me five minutes while I contact the airline?'

'You could do it when you get inside.' Ben's smile

made him look younger than his thirty-eight years. 'Or you could ask me to organise it for you. One of the perks of working a thousand hours a week and enjoying some success is that I have people to do that for me.'

'But I don't,' Millie pointed out.

'While you're with me, you do,' he told her and told his onboard computer to call Einar and, in English this time, asked him to find her a London-bound flight as soon as the airport opened. Einar agreed.

Ben left the car, stood between his open door and her seat and bent his head to meet her eyes. 'When you come back in two weeks, Millie, you will be able to do everything you didn't do this time.'

But Ben would be in St Barth's, so her list of things to do when she returned to Reykjavik wouldn't include sleeping with her husband.

CHAPTER FOUR

'I'M SORRY, I don't understand,' Millie said, looking from an onscreen Olivier to Ben and back to Olivier again.

She sat next to Ben on the couch in his home office. In his home across the city Olivier sat on a couch, his forearms resting on his knees. He was a little older than Ben, dark-haired and dark-eyed.

Ben didn't waste any time explaining to Olivier that they were married, or why they'd married twelve years ago. He simply told Olivier it was time to end their association. Olivier didn't react to Ben's statement and Millie wondered if implacability was a trait that ran through Icelandic veins. What shocked them? She'd loved to know.

'Are you saying that we can't get divorced until we've been legally separated for six months? But we haven't lived together for twelve years! We've *never* lived together!' Millie protested.

'But the state doesn't know that,' Olivier gently told her. 'You need to file a permit notifying that state that you want to get divorced, then proceedings can start. Divorce doesn't happen quickly in Iceland.'

'How long?' Ben asked.

'It usually takes around a year after the period of legal separation has passed. I don't expect it will take that long with you, you have nothing to argue about, but it's best to be prepared.'

Millie groaned. That long? Was she supposed to wait a year before she tried to fall pregnant? No way!

Nobody, least of all Ben, was stopping her from going ahead and making her arrangements to have a baby, but it didn't feel...*right*. Yes, she knew it was silly, theirs was a business arrangement, but she couldn't help the way she felt.

She could, she supposed, carry on with the baby-making process after they were legally separated, but the thought of falling pregnant by someone else— even if he was an anonymous someone!—while she was married to Ben didn't sit well with her. It was silly, she didn't have a relationship with the man, barely knew him, but she still felt as though she couldn't take this next massive step until she'd cut ties with him.

She looked at Olivier. 'And there's no way around that?' she asked, sounding a little desperate.

Olivier looked regretful. 'I'm sorry, but it's the law. I can submit the forms to get the ball rolling in the meantime. Would that be okay?'

What choice did she have? If she wanted to dissolve her marriage, then these were the hoops they needed to jump through. It was annoying, but none of it was Olivier's fault. Or Ben's. She was the one moving the goalposts so she couldn't whine.

She pulled a smile on to her face. 'Yes, please, I'd be grateful for your help.'

Olivier nodded, his dark eyes holding hers. 'If you are dissolving your marriage, does that also mean that you intend to replace Ben as the person managing your trust? If that's the case, then documents need to be filed with the authorities to remove him as a trustee.'

They'd done it before, but Millie had reinstated him a year later.

Ben stiffened. He looked as impenetrable as ever, but she sensed his tension. Locking her fingers together, she shrugged. 'I don't want to,' she admitted. 'Ben has done a marvellous job looking after my investments, but I feel bad asking him to spend time on my—'

'It's a few hours here and there,' Ben interjected. 'I told you, it's not a big deal.'

But Millie couldn't help thinking that if they were going to get divorced, then they should completely split and have nothing to do with each other any more. Divorcing him but still allowing him to run her trust's investments didn't make sense. It would be better if they were either in or out.

Millie told Olivier she'd let him know and, after a few more minutes, Ben disconnected the call. She stood and picked up the glass of red wine he had poured for her earlier and sipped. Holding the glass against her chest, she walked over to the large window and looked out, watching the wild wind bend the trees. A thick layer of snow covered the cars parked on the street and a young man staggered from his car to a house opposite. Millie was relieved when he managed to get his front door open and stumbled into his house.

She remembered days like this from her childhood, but they seemed softer, smudged somehow. There was nothing gentle about what was happening outside. The blizzard raged on, ferocious, elemental… primal. Snow hurtled to the ground, thick and fast, and the curtain of snow allowed only the occasional sighting of cars and trees, lampposts and street signs. The snowflakes were bigger than she'd ever seen before, twirling in the air and smashing into each other.

The wind howled as it whipped the snow and sent it swirling through the air in chaotic, random patterns, and seemed to grow louder and more ferocious by the minute. Ben's street, now impassable—the snow was waist-high in some places—was completely deserted, as anyone with sense was inside, enjoying the warmth and safety of their homes.

Millie couldn't remember when last she had felt so alive. There was something about the wild, uncontrollable aspect of nature, something about being here in Iceland, being with Ben, that made her feel more like the girl she used to be, more like young Millie than the staid Londoner she'd become.

Ben joined her at the window, his big hand wrapped around the bowl of his glass. After showing her where the guest suite was and telling her they were due to talk to Olivier in fifteen minutes, he'd left her to freshen up.

When she found him in his home office, she noticed he'd changed out of his designer suit into dark blue jeans and a bottle-green crew-neck jersey. The soft wool hugged his broad shoulders and showed the definition in his big arms. He looked relaxed and the thought of spending the night in his house, spending alone time with him, made her heart bang against her ribs and her stomach do back flips.

The thought of living with him, even for such a short time, terrified her. Mostly because she didn't know how she was going to keep her clothes on. And her hands off him.

She wanted him, she really, *really* wanted him. And wanting him, in this basic, biblical way, complicated her life in ways she'd never expected. She wasn't supposed to feel desire for her husband, who was nothing much more than a stranger.

Then again, every aspect of her Icelandic trip had gone haywire, so why not this, too?

Their eyes connected. Ben lifted his big hand to hold her cheek and Millie kept her face tipped up, frozen in place. His hand was warm and his big body was now close to hers, radiating heat. She wanted to push her breasts into his chest, her stomach into his hips, she wanted proof he wanted her as much as she wanted him.

She watched as smouldering desire morphed into a blazing wildfire. Any minute now, their clothes would start to fly. She hoped.

'I'm sorry, but I need to kiss you. I can't go another minute without having my mouth on yours, without knowing how you taste.'

There was zero chance of her saying no. Kissing Ben was what she most wanted to do.

He lowered his head and Millie watched his lips descend to hers, and her eyes closed when they touched hers. She lifted her hand to touch his jaw, her fingertips running through his three-day scruff. Her body sank against his as he lightly explored her mouth, his lips moving gently along hers, learning the shape of her lips.

It was a *'hey'* kiss, and a *'so this is how you feel'* kiss. Millie placed her hands flat against his chest and his hand landed on her lower back and he pulled her into him. He kissed her as if he'd finally found what he'd been looking for most of his life, as though she was the biggest, shiniest, loveliest present under the Christmas tree. It was heady stuff to be wanted so much, to feel as though he'd been waiting for months, years, to kiss her like this.

Smart Millie knew he was just a spectacular kisser—she was reading too much into the first meeting of their lips, but she didn't care. It was magical, lovely, fairy footsteps dancing across her soul. Reality would slam into her soon enough. She was happy to take this moment and experience all the feels. Reality could wait.

He smelled of snow and wind, but his cologne reminded her of sunshine and the sea. His body was harder than she expected, more muscled than she'd imagined. He was strong and masculine and felt like a barrier between her and the world. For the first time since her mum died, she didn't feel so utterly alone.

Millie's tongue darted out to touch his lips and Ben stiffened. For a moment Millie thought she'd pushed the kiss too far and asked for too much, too quickly. But then his hand gripped the back of her head and he tugged on her hair, so very gently, silently asking her to tip her head back.

Then he took her mouth in a firestorm of want and need. His tongue slipped between her teeth to slide against hers and Millie, ridiculously, felt her knees melting and her muscles loosening. His hand on her back pulled her into his body and that connection was all that kept her from sinking to the floor.

But her temporary paralysis didn't matter, all that mattered was that Ben was kissing her as though she held all the secrets to the universe and the answers to her most burning questions. And she never, ever, wanted to stop.

Their kiss was as hot as the wind outside was cold. Fireworks flared under her skin and the world faded away, the snowstorm and the howling wind forgotten. Ben placed his hand on her lower back and pulled her to him, her stomach pushing into his oh-so-hard erection, heady proof he wanted her.

Needing her hands on his skin, she pulled his shirt from his pants with rapid tugs and sighed when she encountered the heat of his back, his muscles and the bumps of his spine. She pushed her hand between his back and the band of his pants, frustrated when she couldn't go any further. Their tongues tangled and Ben dialled up the heat by covering her lace-covered breast with his big hand, his thumb swiping across her already hard nipple.

This felt so good, he felt *amazing*. She loved the way he made her feel… Millie wanted more. She wanted everything. Immediately.

Millie reached for his shirt, but she'd barely tugged it an inch upwards when he dropped his hands and yanked his mouth off hers. *What?* Why did he stop? She wanted more…so much more. Their heavy breathing filled the room, interspersed by the screeching wind outside.

Ben ran his hands over his face and tugged his shirt down, and Millie noticed he was a shade paler than he was before. Millie hauled in a deep breath and slowly, oh so slowly, lifted her gaze to meet his. He didn't, thank goodness, look as remote as he normally did. There was a faint flush in his cheeks and his eyes glittered with frustration and need.

He wanted her and their attraction was now an out-of-control wildfire blazing through drought-ravaged forests. For the first time in years, she wanted to fling herself into that firestorm, to taste fire on her tongue. She really wanted a tour of his bedroom. And his bed.

Millie knew how to ask for what she wanted, she was Icelandic enough to be direct. 'Shall we continue things upstairs?'

Ben released a half-laugh, half-snort sound. Was he upset she asked first, because she put what they were both thinking into words? She hoped not, those attitudes were so last century. She was a liberated woman and while she wasn't in the habit of asking guys to sleep with her, she couldn't remember when last she did, she *could*.

She tipped her head to the side. 'I thought that men liked it when a woman takes the lead? You know, less pressure, making it easy?' Right, she was beginning to feel a bit idiotic, as though she'd mis-read the situation. She might be liberated, but she was very out of practice. Had she done something wrong? Gone too fast? Come on too strong? What?

'Right, since you're not tugging me up the stairs, I presume that's not something you want to do.' She threw up her hands and pulled a face. 'So what do we do now?'

His gaze, as it so often was, was steady and sin-cerity replaced lust.

'Now, we take a breather and I see what I can find to feed you. When last did you eat?'

Really? How was she supposed to think about food when he was all she wanted to feast on? Mil-lie rubbed her hands over her face. She'd had a cup of coffee on the plane and hadn't eaten breakfast.

'How did we go from a hot kiss to talking about food?' she asked, puzzled.

He sighed. 'Millie, you're in my house, through necessity, not by choice. I don't want you to feel pres-surised or coerced into doing anything you don't want to. I kissed you, that's as far as I'll go.'

'But I told you I wanted—'

She tipped her head to the side, silently waiting

for him to explain. After lifting his hands and dropping them in an I-don't-know-what-I'm-doing gesture, he spoke again. 'Look, I never expected to be this attracted to you. Wanting my wife was the last thing I expected and I'm feeling a bit off balance. I expect you are, too.'

Unbalanced? No, she felt as though she'd been sideswiped by an avalanche.

His thick eyebrows pulled together. 'It's been a long, strange day, a puzzling one. We haven't seen each other for more than a decade and we've been thrown into sharing my house for a day, maybe more. We're getting divorced, you want a baby. We both want to see each other naked. What was once a simple deal is now complicated.'

His sensible words obliterated her impulsiveness. Millie folded her arms and rocked on her heels, feeling a little embarrassed and, dammit, grateful. While she'd been happy to skip into the inferno, he'd looked beyond their hot-as-the-inside-of-the-sun attraction to consider the consequences. She'd been impetuous, he thoughtful.

Millie wished she could argue with him, but she couldn't. It *had* been an exceptionally weird day. And now, below the lust, the longing, a streak of hesitation pulsed, a layer of should she, shouldn't she? She'd felt off balance all day and was old enough to know it wasn't a good time to step on to a sexual merry-go-round. Nothing good came out of impulsively throwing yourself into a man's arms…

'Right, point taken,' Millie admitted.

'I'm backing off because it's the right thing to do right now, Millie. But if you decide I'm what you want later, you just have to ask, and I'll have your clothes off so fast your head will spin.'

Millie blinked, letting his words sink in. Getting the firestorm that they created inside her under control.

'I'm going to head to the kitchen and distract myself by looking for something to eat for supper.'

'Ben—' Millie sighed. She didn't want him to go, he couldn't stay. She wanted him to kiss her again. She needed to find her room and take a sanity break.

She was supposed to be breaking their ties, not forging new ones. She'd come to Iceland to close the book, to put her past on the shelf, to move on.

She had to be a sensible adult.

Divorce, pregnancy, baby, a new life, her own little family. She'd made her plan—there was no space for a brief affair with her never there, stranger-husband. Ben wouldn't be a part of her future, no man would.

She needed to keep it together, to consider the future. Sleeping with him would be instant gratification, a wonderful step out of time, but it could have… unintended consequences. Ben was a potent man and she'd kissed him and propositioned him, something that normally took her weeks to do with other men. She was acting out of character and needed time and space to clear her head and start thinking clearly.

There was a blizzard outside and a bigger one happening inside her head.

She had to back off, with as much dignity as she

could manage. 'You're right, with me wanting a divorce, and a baby, it's too complicated, too messy,' Millie told him. She bit the inside of her lip. 'Sorry, I lost my head.'

'Don't apologise, Millie, it's not necessary,' Ben said and she heard regret in his voice. 'Our marriage was once a very simple arrangement. Now it's... n-not.'

She looked out of the window, hoping against hope that the storm had cleared and she could leave, find somewhere else to stay. But, no—if anything, the blizzard was just getting started. She was stuck here, feeling awkward and sexually frustrated. Not a great combination.

'I'm sorry if all of this has inconvenienced you, Benedikt. I would go if I could.'

'I'll be in the kitchen...give me a half-hour or so. When *you* are ready, join me.'

Millie nodded, understanding his need for some space. She needed that time, possibly more, for Sensible Millie to slap Turned On Millie back into shape.

Sleeping with Ben would be a ghastly mistake. But there was still nothing she wanted to do more.

In his kitchen, Ben heard her on the stairs as she made her way up to the guest suite. Running his hand through his hair, he walked over to a kitchen cupboard and yanked out a bottle and a shot glass. It might be a little early for alcohol—it was only two in the afternoon—but he desperately needed a drink.

After swallowing a shot of Brennivín, his Icelandic father's favourite drink, he placed the empty glass against his forehead and closed his eyes.

Millie was upstairs, in one of the three spare bedrooms, and she was going to be sleeping in that bed tonight, tomorrow night. And he'd told her that nothing would happen between them...

Unless she asked.

Ben walked over to the window and placed his shoulder against the window frame and watched the wind toss big, feathery snowflakes on to the glass. The wind screamed its fury outside, and Ben could barely make out the huge branches of the trees in his garden and couldn't see the gate or the street. The blizzard was causing chaos and disorientation outside. Millie did the same inside his mind. Ben was fairly certain both storms were going to intensify.

It had been obvious Millie wanted to leave after the dust settled on their kiss and, had there been a way, he would've helped her go. But the snow was thigh deep, the visibility impenetrable, the roads were undrivable and the wind strong enough to blow trucks off the road. This wasn't weather you took chances in, it was supremely dangerous out there.

It was marginally less dangerous inside his house, for vastly different reasons. He and Millie were snowbound, forced to share the same house. If she were another woman he was attracted to, he'd consider it a perfect situation. With the storm raging, he wouldn't be able to go into the office and he could spend long, lazy hours in bed, having sex, giving and receiving pleasure. He couldn't remember when last, if ever, he had three days of uninterrupted time with a lover...

But the woman upstairs wasn't just someone he was head-over-ass attracted to, but his wife of twelve years. His attraction to her was stunning, and inconvenient, mostly because he didn't like how out of control Millie made him feel. He looked at her and he wanted, he touched her and he burned. He never dated women who made him feel more than a passing attraction, interest, who made him tip his head, intrigued. He ran, as far and as fast as he could. Millie made him feel all that and more and there was no damn place to run to, no way of putting some distance between them.

For the past two decades, sex had been a tool for pleasure, fun and a way to burn away stress. It had never been preceded by such need and constant thoughts of having her and how he would take her. Millie had been back in his life for a few hours, but the storm in his head matched the ferocity of the blizzard outside. She was a hurricane rushing through his soul, a tornado spinning through his mind. He wasn't quite sure which way was up...

Absurd!

He wasn't a man who allowed himself to get carried away, he prided himself on being rational and calm. He didn't believe in love or excess emotion, he knew it always led to hurt and disappointment.

The woman he'd allowed himself to love had let him down and there was no way he'd allow that to happen again. He'd worked exceptionally hard to become the emotionally independent, sometimes ruthless, impassive man he now was and he'd never put himself at the mercy of needing a woman's love again. Emotional distance and not allowing himself to have feelings of attachment to anything—not to money or people or things—gave him a sense of freedom and security.

Staying away from emotional situations also kept his stutter at bay.

Yes, he'd hesitated once or twice, and felt the prickles in his throat when his words took longer than usual to appear. But that could be due to stress, to the surprise of Millie dropping back into his life. There was nothing to worry about; he hadn't spent enough time with Millie to know whether she could sneak under his defences, whether she was able to burrow her way inside his steel-hard carapace and look past his carefully constructed veneer of implacability.

But he had to be careful of her, he couldn't start feeling more, feeling *anything* for his on-paper wife. And he knew he shouldn't sleep with her...

He needed a good excuse to spend time away from her. Work would work and he could spend more time in his basement gym.

Ben tapped his empty glass against his thigh, his attention moving to what Olivier had said about their divorce. He had no problem with waiting to get divorced, it wasn't a problem for him.

But he'd seen Millie's look of horror and knew the waiting period would derail her plans to have a baby. She didn't want to start this new chapter of her life until the ties were cut between them. He could understand that. He believed, like Millie did, that a clean break should be made before one moved on…

She wanted a child and he could see her with a baby. She had so much love to give and, like her mother, was warm and affectionate. Millie would be an exceptional mother, and he wanted that for her. He wanted her to be happy. But despite trying, he was finding it difficult to wrap his head around her using a sperm donor to fall pregnant.

Yes, yes, it was the modern way of doing things, a choice she had the absolute right to make—her body and her choice—but it just felt…*wrong*.

He couldn't explain it, he just didn't *like* it.

But he was also bemused by her deep desire to have a child.

Unlike her, he'd never given a lot of thought, if any, to procreation and the urge to do so wasn't innate. It was easy to find excuses—there were enough kids in the world as it was, he had no time, his career was his primary focus.

Nothing, as far as he was concerned, was missing in his life, he didn't see how kids would fit in with his schedule, the little free time he had or the life he'd worked his tail off to attain.

Millie wanted children, but he didn't. He was attracted to her, she was a gorgeous woman, and he was a man with normal sexual desires. He liked women and liked to sleep with them. It was a fun, completely normal urge.

And if she was anyone other than his wife, and his business partner, if he wasn't involved with making the financial decisions about her vast investments, he wouldn't think twice about spending the next two days in bed with her, naked.

But she was his wife, the wife who wanted a divorce so she could have a baby. They co-owned a company and he'd offered to continue to handle her trust's huge investment portfolio. They were already dealing with a lot and sleeping together would be a flame inserted into a gas line.

He'd worked exceptionally hard to get where he was, to have the career and business he enjoyed, to find the ninety/ten balance between work and play. He liked his life, sometimes he even loved it. He couldn't allow his no-longer-convenient wife to upset it. He had to be sensible, he should avoid complications…

But he really hoped she would ask.

CHAPTER FIVE

AFTER SPENDING TWO nights in Ben's wonderful house, Millie was starting to climb the walls. Despite using the state-of-the-art gym in his basement she wanted to breathe fresh air, go for a walk and to put some space between them.

Living with someone she was so desperately attracted to wasn't, in any way, fun and staying in a hotel's broom closet might've been a better idea. Being housebound was a lot easier for Ben, he had work to do, and he spent hours in his downstairs study doing whatever the CEO of PR Reliance International did. He didn't have time to sit around wondering how it would feel to have his hands on her body, the scrape of her leg against his, his big hands lifting her up as he slid into her...

Aargh! Honestly?

Millie picked the magazine she'd been reading and frisbee'd it across the room in a fit of pique. Ben chose that moment to walk into the smaller of his two reception rooms and the magazine slammed into his thigh. His only reaction was to lift his eyebrows. He picked up the magazine and placed it on the nearest side table. 'Problem?' he asked.

Millie blushed, swung her sock-covered feet off the couch, leaned forward and placed her forearms on her knees. She hoped her hair dropping on either side of her face would hide her flaming cheeks. She was acting like a stroppy child.

After tossing another log in the fireplace, Ben sat next to her and pulled back a hank of hair and tucked it behind her ear. A soft, sky-blue cashmere blanket fell to the floor. 'Have you got cabin fever?' he asked.

She shrugged, not willing to admit she was suffering from I-want-to-sleep-with-him fever more than any other ailment. 'Yes,' she admitted.

'This is the worst storm we've had this decade,' Ben told her, leaning back. He smothered a yawn and rested his head on the back of the couch and closed his eyes. His thick eyelashes rested against the faint blue stripes beneath his eyes—he was more tired than she'd realised. Wasn't he sleeping?

Why?

'Tough day?' she asked, shuffling back and lifting her feet on to the couch, then wrapping her arms around her bent knees.

'No more than usual,' he told her, rolling his head in her direction before opening his eyes. 'Why?'

'You look tired. And stressed,' she stated, allowing herself the pleasure of tracing the darkness under his eyes with the tip of her index finger. Touching him was a compulsion and she was tired of holding herself back.

His eyes didn't drop from hers, holding her gaze.

'I'm not sleeping because I spend most of the night talking myself out of walking down the hallway and slipping into your bed.'

Icelandic people were generally blunt—it was a trait she had taken to London with her when she left. She liked knowing where she stood. After her mum's lies about her father and Magnús's cold deceit—if she hadn't pushed his buttons so hard and so often, she probably would still think *he* was her father—honesty was a refreshing and welcome change. And Millie recalled his promise to her. He would never lie to her. As far as she knew, he hadn't.

If he did, she'd find his deceit devastating. In a world full of shifting opinions and fake news, she'd relied on him to tell her the truth about the business, her investments and the trust's business.

'I've been doing the same,' she admitted and managed a small smile. 'It would've been kind of funny if we met in the hallway rushing to each other's rooms, wouldn't it?'

Ben's intensity didn't waver and wasn't distracted by her weak joke. 'Since you arrived, I've been trying to talk myself out of taking you to bed, praying you'd cave and ask me again. We're both single and we want each other. Why are we denying ourselves something we both know we're going to enjoy?'

She swallowed. 'Because we're married? Because if we sleep together, it will change things. It will affect our arrangement,' she said, the heat in his eyes raising the temperature of the already warm room.

'I've been thinking about that,' he mused. 'How would it affect anything? We've never allowed other lovers to affect our marriage deal—what difference would it make if we are each other's lovers?'

'I don't know!' Millie rubbed her hands over her face. 'Ben, this isn't helping!'

'We're trying to dissolve our…arrangement,' he pointed out. 'But our attraction to each other has nothing to do with the deal we struck, the dissolution of that deal. It's a separate issue.'

Was it? To her, everything was jumbled up. She felt as though she was in an industrial washing machine, being tumbled this way and that. Sex, baby, their marriage, being business partners…they all bled into each other.

Ben didn't move from his indolent position, but every muscle in his body was on high alert. He was waiting for her to say the word and he would take control. She was so close to saying yes and words like *please love me…take me to bed* and *I want you* hovered on her tongue, desperate to be verbalised.

'We can get the divorce you want and I'll stay on as your trustee if that's what you want. Your wanting a child doesn't, so you've said, c-c-concern me—'

She'd caught his sporadic, barely-there stutter and found the small imperfection charming. And reassuring because Ben sometimes seemed too together, too polished. His infrequent stammer made him seem a little fallible.

'But, more than anything else, I want to take you to bed,' he continued.

Millie hesitated and Ben caught it. He sat up, his expression serious. 'This will only become complicated if we let it, Millie. This has nothing to do with our arrangement or our divorce.'

'It's about the way we feel when we look at each other,' Millie murmured. She'd never had a man look at her with such intensity, as though she was all he needed for him to keep breathing, and existing.

To be desired by someone so much was a heady experience and it was something Millie doubted she'd feel again. Ben was such a *man*, masculine and hot, and to know that someone so sexy wanted her flooded her with a confidence she couldn't remember feeling.

She was done with thinking, finished with denying herself what she really wanted. Ben was right— this didn't need to be complicated.

'This is about sex, a fling, a step out of time,' Millie quietly stated. 'It can't mean anything.'

Ben nodded. 'So…can I kiss you now?'

Millie looked temptation in the eye, nodded her agreement and followed it over to the dark side. She wanted him, he wanted her, this was going to happen…

Millie dropped her knees and moved to straddle Ben's lap. His hands came up to hold her hips and surprise, then delight, flashed in his eyes. Millie pulled up his black cashmere sweater and placed her hands on the bare skin of his stomach, felt his muscles tighten beneath her fingertips.

She lowered her mouth to kiss him, but Ben's

whisper stopped her before she could make contact. 'Are you sure you want this, Millie? Because once we start, I'm not sure I'll be able to stop.'

Of course he would, of that she had no doubt. Ben was a man who exuded control, over his actions and words. She absolutely knew he would stop if she asked him to. But she had no intention of stopping before he gave her an earth-moving orgasm. Or two or three. She wanted to know what making love to this amazing man felt like. 'I'm sure, Ben.'

She remembered him saying that she needed to ask him to kiss her, to make love to her, so she decided to say the words, to leave him in no doubt. 'Will you take me to bed, Ben? Will you love me?'

He lifted his hand and, with one finger, traced the curve of her cheek, the line of her jaw. 'Does it have to be in my bed?' he asked. 'This couch and the carpet in front of the fireplace are incredibly comfortable and I can't wait that long.'

She smiled, her lips curving as her hands skimmed over his pectorals. 'We can start here and make our way upstairs as the night progresses.'

'That,' Ben said, between kissing her lips, 'sounds like a very good plan.'

They were doing this. He closed his eyes as Millie's hands danced over his ribs and he shivered. All he could do was echo her actions, so he pushed his hands under the hem of her long-sleeved silk T-shirt. His fingers moved slowly up her ribcage and flirted with the sides of her full breasts. He ran his thumb over her nipple, rasping over the lace cup of her bra. She felt so incredibly good… Amazing, feminine and completely delightful.

He banded an arm around her waist, lifted her up and off him and slowly, so slowly, lowered her to the cushions of the couch. He smiled at the combination of excitement and desire on her face and her grape-green eyes seemed lighter and brighter than they normally were. She wanted him…she'd *asked* him.

He lowered his mouth to hers, sucking on her bottom lip, then sliding his tongue into her mouth. Her hands skimmed his sides and she dug her fingers into his butt, her hands sliding as far down the back of his thighs as she could reach. Lifting her hands, she placed them on either side of his face and the combination of that sexy, tender gesture nearly undid him. Millie pulled her mouth off his and ran her tongue over his jaw, down his neck and, after pulling the neck of his T-shirt away, dragged her teeth over his collarbone.

'You feel amazing…you're so sexy,' she murmured.

Ben couldn't remember when last he was complimented, in bed or out. He tugged on the hem of her T-shirt, a silent plea to remove the barriers of clothing between them. Millie did as he asked and tossed the shirt over the back of the couch. Ben took a minute to take in creamy breasts nestled in a deep purple bra.

Millie arched her back and he knew she was quietly begging him to touch her, to pay attention to her nipples. Ben was happy to oblige. He dropped his head and sucked one into his mouth, lace and all, and she released a deep, appreciative groan. Her fingers tunnelled into his hair, gripping his head to keep him in place.

She was what he'd craved since the moment he saw her yesterday, the reason why he couldn't sleep. When he did drift off, making love to her was what he dreamed of—he'd wanted these moments—he craved the ebb and tide of hot, delicious sex. Ben needed to touch her everywhere and he wanted her to know him, to explore him in the same way he intended to explore her.

She would be returning to the UK soon and when she next returned to Iceland, he'd be in St Barth's. He didn't know when, or if, he'd see her next. If this was the only time they had, if this night was all they got, he wanted to know her inside out, what made her sigh and what made her scream. And he wanted her to know him, to remember him…

He wanted to be her only memory when sex slid into her mind…

But as he touched her, as his mouth moved down her body to explore her belly button, to drag his warm, open mouth over her mound, he knew he could, if he wasn't careful, become addicted to her, to this. She could become something he couldn't get enough of.

She was skimming in and out of his life, and soon, the fragile ties that bound them would be broken. She wasn't for ever, he didn't do that long. He wasn't into commitment, of any length or any type. This was about pleasure, nothing more. And if he kept telling himself that, maybe he would, at some point, start to believe it.

Ben divested Millie of her underwear and, sitting on his heels, he looked at her, gorgeously naked. He was entranced by her delightful body, her long, shapely legs and her creamy, scented skin. 'You are exquisite, Millie.'

Millie's eyes darkened, her lips curled up and she sighed, but her eyes didn't leave his. Although he wanted to kiss her more than he wanted to breathe, Ben kept his eyes on her face and watched emotions slide in and out of her startling eyes and across her face. Lust, desire, crazy attraction—they were all there, but he thought that under the want was affection, a little fear and a lot of anticipation.

He wanted to remind her, remind himself, that romance had no part in this. This was about sex and escapism. They were doing what women and men did best...

Ben pulled away from her and lifted his hand to grip the back of his shirt. He pulled it over his head in one easy, fluid movement. Millie growled and ran her hand over his chest, lightly touched with hair. He flipped open the buttons to his jeans, hooked his thumbs into the waistband and pushed his jeans down his thighs, taking his underwear with them.

The sigh that followed was one of pure female appreciation.

Naked, Ben gripped her waist and moved her down the couch. When she was where he wanted her, he lay down on top of her, chest to chest, his erection finding its natural place between her thighs. Wanting more, he pulled back to kiss his way down her neck, across her collarbone. She was so lovely, and he couldn't get enough of her. He pulled her nipple into his mouth and her fingers twisted in his hair. She liked that, seemed to like everything he did. She was so damn hot...

He was so close to making her his...one little push and he'd be in heaven. But...*aargh*! He needed a condom or Millie would be getting that baby sooner than she thought.

He looked up and pushed a strand of hair from her face. She gripped his hips and dropped her legs open. Ben groaned and shook his head.

'What's the matter?' she whispered, immediately tensing. He saw the vulnerability in her eyes—she thought he was slamming on the brakes. There wasn't a remote chance of that happening.

'I need to get a condom, sweetheart. I'll be back in a sec.'

Ben reluctantly pulled away from her. He knew he had a condom in his wallet, which lay on the hallway table, just outside the door to this lounge. He moved quickly and came back into the room, scattering cards and cash over the intricate parquet floor as he searched for the condom he'd shoved into one of the compartments a few months back. Finally digging it out, he ripped it open, sheathed himself and lowered himself back down to the couch, settling himself back between her thighs.

Ben kissed her gently before skimming his thumb over the spot between her eyes. 'Second thoughts?' he asked. He wanted her, wanted this more than anything he'd ever wanted before, but he needed to know whether she felt the same. If she didn't, his withered heart might just crack…

Her ankles were already curved around his calves, and she was lifting her hips, trying to push him deeper into her. 'No, but I'm tired of waiting. I *need* you.'

Oh, he liked her like this, a little breathless, hunger in her eyes, her body pushing up into his, wanting what he could give her. He deliberately brushed his chest against hers, teasing her nipples with his chest hair. Unfortunately, his teasing backfired and he knew he couldn't wait much longer to make her his. He was running out of patience.

'Quick question?' she asked.

His eyes bored into her. 'Make it very damn quick.'

'I was just wondering how long you are going to tease me?'

'This long.' Ben entered her with one fluid stroke, burying himself to the hilt. Yeah, this was what he loved, what he craved, being encased by a woman, enveloped in her heat and scent, feeling her lift her hips in a silent but powerful demand for him to go deeper, to take her harder. Then Millie lifted her mouth to find his and Ben forgot how to think.

All he could concentrate on was the warm, sparkly sensation building in a place deep inside him, each spark igniting another until a million tiny fires danced under his skin. Ben placed his hand under her back, yanked her up and he pushed deeper into her, and those fires joined and created an explosion that consumed him from the inside out. All he wanted was this heat and light and warmth. Her. He wanted *her*. This. Again and again and again.

Millie's internal muscles clenched around him, he felt her wet gush against him and heard her sob his name. He'd had good sex before, great sex often. But this was better, hotter, brighter. And that, Ben thought as followed Millie into that white-hot, blinding rush of sensation, was a huge problem.

Much, much later, after Ben had loved her thoroughly and exquisitely again, Millie heard the sound of his deep breathing and watched him in the low light coming from his spectacular en-suite bathroom. Millie lifted his big hand off her bare stomach and held her breath, waiting for him to wake up. He didn't, so she slipped out of his enormous bed and picked up one of his long-sleeved T-shirts lying on the back of the chair in the corner of his spacious room. She pulled it over her head, rolled up the sleeves and, after finding her panties and pulling them on, padded downstairs, needing to be alone.

She approved of Ben's renovated, now contemporary, split-level house, with all the levels arranged around the original, central courtyard. All the rooms had parquet floors, high ceilings and big windows, letting in as much natural light as possible. She loved its layout, and its decor, not overly minimalistic, and she felt at home.

Moving down the steps, Millie walked into the kitchen area with its mahogany cupboards, granite counters and stainless-steel appliances. A big island dominated the room and to the left was a spacious, casual eating area under a massive window. The built-in, L-shaped couch half framed the dining table and it was wide enough to sleep on.

Millie took a bottle of water from the fridge and cracked the top, took a long swallow and looked out, sighing at the still-falling snow. She needed a few minutes to make sense of what had happened upstairs and to get her brain to restart. If that took a while, she wouldn't be surprised—she felt as though she'd been hit by a massive power surge.

She'd had a few lovers over the years, but sex with those men couldn't compare to what she'd experienced with Ben. He was a tender and thorough lover and he'd shown her how fantastic sex could be. It was an eye-opener to realise she'd only ever had boring sex, mediocre sex and okay sex. Making love to Ben was a transformative experience and she'd never be satisfied with anything less than brilliant sex again.

That shouldn't be a problem because, after she left Reykjavik, her focus would move from having a lover to acquiring a baby. She doubted she'd be interested in sex while she was pregnant and, after the baby was born, all her focus would be on her child. Hopefully, by the time she finally turned her attention back to her own sexual needs, the memory of this incredible night spent in Ben's arms, and how brilliant he was in bed, would've dissipated.

Millie sat on one of the bar stools at the island and crossed her bare legs. She pulled her laptop towards her—she'd left it here earlier—and switched it on. They'd had sex, it had been stunning and amazing, but she had to put it into perspective: it was a fling, not destined to last. It didn't matter that she wanted more than one delicious night, wasn't important that she needed more of his growled compliments, to hear his murmurs of appreciation at how fantastic she made him feel.

He'd made her feel more like a woman, fierce and fantastic, than she ever had before, but where did that get her? The harsh reality was that there was nothing more between them than a once-convenient marriage and pheromones.

Unfortunately, she hadn't expected to like him so much. They'd both had good reasons to marry back then—she to get her stepfather out of her life, he to get her stepfather out of the company. Things ticked along happily until her biological clock started setting off alarm bells...

Millie wondered if Ben had ever wanted kids, if having a family was something he'd ever considered. She knew little about his family and wondered why he'd never married or had a long-term partner. If he had, she would know about it, it was part of their pact to be honest with each other.

Ben, she suspected, was married to the company and his career. He'd taken the business to unimaginable heights, making them both—well, him and her mum's foundation, because that's where her share of the company profits ended up—exceptionally rich. Success like that required pinpoint focus and dedication.

But, for some mad reason, she could see him married, see him as a dad. She could easily imagine him standing at that stove, dressed in a T-shirt and plaid pyjama pants, his feet bare as he flipped pancakes for his toddler son and dropped kisses on the head of his flaxen-haired daughter. His lower face would be rough with stubble, his usually neat hair would be messy, and happiness and contentment would make him look younger than his years. He'd smile when she walked through the door...

Whoa, brakes on, Millie!

Too much and too fast. Ben wasn't going to be her happy-ever-after, because she didn't believe her happiness rested in a man's hands. And she had too many trust issues to let a man that far into her world and heart. Ben would never be the man she created a family with, the man she'd spend the rest of her life with. There wasn't going to *be* a man. No, it was better to be a single mum and not risk her heart.

She was going to have her family, and it would be just her and her kids. And the donor of the biological matter she needed would be anonymous. If her kids wanted to know who he was, and if he was open to that, they could track him down when they were adults, but she never wanted a relationship with the man.

Stop thinking about Ben and start thinking about your Ben-free future, Millie!

Now, or some time very soon, she had to work out when to get pregnant. But before she did that, she had to get past her reluctance to fall pregnant while she was still married to Ben. It was stupid to wait up to eighteen months to get pregnant because she felt 'uncomfortable' about being married to Ben while carrying another man's child.

She wasn't properly married to Ben and the baby would be hers. Neither man would play a part in her or her baby's life going forward so she was being incredibly stupid. She had to get over herself. Immediately.

She needed to get serious about finding a sperm donor, so she opened her laptop and pulled up the website of the sperm bank she favoured using. Millie idly scrolled through the website. If she and Ben got divorced shortly after their government-imposed, six-month waiting period, then she could have the baby any time after July next year. It made sense to start trying to fall pregnant in the New Year, as her first attempt might not be successful.

Derek is a super-smart, persistent and very kind man with a fun, open personality. He also has gorgeous blue eyes and light brown hair, with impressive cheekbones and a straight nose. He's on an impressive career path, has two degrees, in genetics and pharmacology, and wants to establish his own bio lab to tailor-make drugs to individuals. Derek has a large family he is close to...

Admittedly, Derek looked sexy and athletic, but Millie wanted to know more. Did he sulk? Was he the type to lose his temper? Did he make promises he didn't keep? Millie sighed. She could never fill in all the blanks—nobody could, not even in a proper relationship—but she wanted to know more, dig deeper. This was someone who would pass on a hefty chunk of his genes to her baby, she wanted to know the good, the bad and the ugly.

How was she supposed to make a choice when she didn't know *everything*?

Millie looked out of the large windows that were a feature of Ben's open plan living area and sighed at the endlessly falling snow, wondering when the wind would ever stop howling. She felt tired but energised, sleepy but her mind was on a spin cycle.

'He sounds too good to be true.'

Millie slapped her hand on her chest and spun around to see Ben standing by the island, his eyes on her computer screen. Yawning, he scratched the side of his neck and walked towards the enormous fridge. He removed a bottle of orange juice, slammed the door closed with his foot and took a glass from the cupboard next to the fridge. He downed a tall glass of orange juice before refilling the glass and coming to stand next to her.

'Should I be offended that you are looking for sperm donors after we nearly set the house on fire?' he asked, his tone mild. He stroked his hand over her hair and she responded by lifting her face, silently and subconsciously, asking for a kiss. His lips met hers with gentle heat.

'They are separate issues,' Millie quietly reminded him. 'I still want a baby and I'm not going to get one until I decide who I want the sperm donor to be.'

'So what's the problem?' Ben asked, sitting next to her and placing his forearm on the counter. He'd pulled on a pair of sweatpants and a T-shirt and, yes, his big feet were bare. He looked like the man she'd imagined earlier, the one flipping pancakes...

Stop it, Millie!

'I can choose everything: hair colour, eye colour, height and build. His ethnicity,' Millie explained, pushing her hands into her hair. And, yes, it felt weird discussing this with him. 'But I can't tell what sort of personality he has. How does he react to stress? To hardship? Is he a bully or is he sensitive?' Magnús's face popped up on the big screen of her mind. 'Does he have a temper? Does he say one thing and do another?'

'Are you thinking about how Magnús treated you? If you are, then you are giving him too much power,' Ben told her.

Millie silently cursed, wishing he wouldn't read her mind. Maybe she'd told him too much earlier. Why had she told him about Magnús's hatred towards her because she'd never shared that with anyone?

Not even her mum understood how much Magnús detested her. Millie had always sensed his dislike, but didn't understand how deep his hatred ran until their big blowout. He resented having to raise her, resented the attention her mum paid her, resented her mum's insistence that he claim her as his.

Why had they both promoted the lie? Iceland was an accepting society and having a child by someone else wasn't that big a deal, even thirty years ago. Millie didn't understand their motives and she definitely didn't understand why they'd kept her real father's identity a secret.

There would be no lies in her family, no secrets. Her children would, when they were old enough to understand, know everything about her and her family.

'To be fair, most couples take years to know each other that well,' he stated. 'It's not something you can discover in a few conversations.'

It took her a minute to work out that Ben was referring to her statement about not knowing the ins and outs of her potential sperm donor.

Funny that Ben was the person she'd known the longest, the man who'd been on the outside of her life for most of her life. A spark of an idea flared in the deepest part of her.

Ben had been amazing these past twelve years. He was always polite, always calm and he'd made great decisions for the company and her. She trusted him. He was smart, good looking and healthy, and making a baby with him would be so much more fun than the soulless clinic visit she was anticipating.

The spark flared into a flame. Had she found

a neat solution to her dilemma? He'd married her, they were business partners and now they were lovers, possibly even on their way to being friends. She hadn't come across anyone on the website of sperm donors who could match him.

'You're plotting something,' Ben said, resting his forearms on the counter. Her eyes darted back to the website and then to him and back to the website again. When fear jumped into his eyes, she knew he'd worked out what she was thinking...

'You can't possibly be thinking that I...' He stopped talking, still shaking his head.

'That I would like you to be my father's baby?' Millie looked him in the eye and nodded. He'd be perfect. Well, not perfect, but miles better than anyone on any website.

Ben linked his hands behind his head, still calm. Would she ever be able to surprise him? She doubted it. 'That's a chemical reaction to us having great sex, Millie.'

Was it? She didn't think so. She knew Ben, she trusted him. She liked him. They'd already slept together. 'Nobody comes close to you on the sperm donor website, Ben.'

He shot a look at her laptop and Millie closed the lid.

'I cannot believe that you are asking this,' Ben muttered. Millie frowned. Right. Her request might not be a surprise, but it wasn't a welcome one. 'I don't want to be a father, I never planned on having kids.'

Millie frowned at him. Oh, damn! He'd grabbed

the wrong end of the stick and was impaled on the sharp point.

She lifted her hand and shook her head. 'Whoa, hold on! I'm not asking you to be involved in his, or her, life.'

'Th-then what are you asking, Millie?'

She fully intended to raise her baby alone, without anyone's input. This baby, and its sibling, if she was lucky enough to be able to do this again, would be her family, she would be a single parent and responsible for raising her child. She didn't want any outside input, thank you very much. Her body, her baby…

'I don't want a *father* for my baby, Benedikt, that's not what I'm asking. I intend to raise this baby on my own. All I'd require is for you to help me become pregnant. I still want a divorce. I wouldn't expect you to pay me maintenance or to be involved in my child's life. I'd happily sign any legal documents stating that.'

'So you just want my sperm?' he clarified, with a strange look on his face.

She lifted one shoulder to her ear. 'Yes.'

'I'm not sure whether to feel relieved or insulted,' Ben stated. Millie couldn't read the emotion in his eyes and she didn't like it when he closed down mentally and emotionally. Looking closely, she saw that there was heat within those blue depths, as well as irritation. She bit down on her bottom lip.

Had she completely spoiled what had been a lovely night by tossing this idea into the equation? Possibly. Probably. But she wasn't good at waiting for what she wanted. Once she decided to embark on a course of action she jumped in with both feet and her whole body.

Millie twisted her lips. 'I'm sorry, I've thrown this at you late at night and after…after we just had an amazing time together in bed.'

Ben sent her one of his enigmatic looks, the one where she had no idea what he was thinking and feeling. Millie felt like an absolute fool…and wasn't sure what to do. She'd erected this huge barrier between them—she'd couldn't flip back into being his lover…

Why hadn't she thought more and spoken less? 'Uh…so I'm going to go to bed.'

What else could she say? Do? She hesitated a minute and hoped Ben would say something to reduce the tension between them, to take them back to where they were a few hours ago. She'd messed up and she was hoping *he'd* get her out of her jam. She wasn't being fair…

'I am sorry, Ben. Having a baby is important to me and…' she said, feeling the need to explain.

When his eyes remained steady on her face, she knew she was digging her hole deeper and making the situation a lot worse. Thank God he'd worn a condom tonight; her falling pregnant accidentally was the last thing she wanted. She would never take the decision out of his hands and she hoped he knew that. She thought about reminding him of that and decided not to, it would only make the situation worse.

Ben released a long, drawn-out sigh and rubbed the back of his neck. 'Go to bed, Millie.'

There was nothing else she could do, nothing else she could say, so she did as he suggested. She climbed the stairs to the guest bedroom, knowing she'd spend the rest of the night, not that there was much of it left, cursing herself for asking him to be her baby daddy.

And praying for a miracle he would agree.

CHAPTER SIX

THERE WAS FLIPPING things upside down and then there were emotional nuclear strikes.

When Ben followed Millie downstairs he'd expected maybe a whisky-flavoured hot chocolate in the kitchen, running his hands up her bare legs as they watched the still-falling snow through his huge windows.

He had not been expecting her to ask him to give her a baby.

Ben opened a cupboard door, pulled out a bottle of whisky sans hot chocolate and reached for a glass. Dumping a healthy amount into the glass, he threw it back, welcoming the heat as it slipped down his throat. He started to pour himself another shot and stopped, thinking that alcohol would not add any clarity to the situation.

He walked over to the L-shaped couch in the corner of the kitchen, underneath the wide, tall windows, lay down and rested his head on a cushion, with his forearm over his eyes.

The sex they shared had been brilliant and he'd

enjoyed feeling completely in sync with another person. Millie had been as into him as he was her and they seemed to be reading from the same book, singing the same tune. He instinctively knew how to touch her, what she'd like and didn't. She hadn't been shy about exploring his body and she'd paid attention to his responses. In some ways, it felt as though they'd made love a hundred times before, yet coming together was still new and exhilarating.

She'd rocked his world and he knew he'd returned that favour. They'd had simple, uncomplicated, unbelievably amazing sex...*twice*. And he'd thought they'd spend the rest of the night having more brilliant sex. But her question changed their dynamic in a heartbeat.

Could he give her a child?

Wow. And what the hell? He had no idea how he'd managed to keep so calm, to not react. Maybe he'd been too shocked to react.

He wasn't sure whether to be irritated by her question, hurt or annoyed.

Ben dropped his arm, sat up and glanced out of the window. Still snowing...*dammit*. The usual sounds of his busy street were drowned out by the snow-filled wind. The dim street lights cast long, distorted shadows on the snowbanks, creating an eerie atmosphere.

Ben tipped his head back to look up at the ceiling. On the next floor, somewhere directly above him, Millie slept. He rubbed his hands over his face. On his *What-will-Millie-do-next?* bingo card, getting her pregnant didn't feature. He'd married her to protect his business interests and he'd looked after her interests, and the personal trust she'd inherited from Jacqui, as he would his own money. Giving her a baby wasn't part of that agreement.

He didn't want to be a father and had never had any interest in raising a child. He had no idea how to juggle a kid and a career and was scared to try because his mum had been so shockingly bad at being a mother and having a career. And, thanks to his mum being difficult about visitation rights—she didn't want him to stay with her, but she didn't want him to spend time with his dad either—he and his Icelandic father had had a cordial, but not particularly close, relationship.

He hadn't had a decent role model, nobody to teach him how to be a good parent. His mother had veered from thinking he was mildly intellectually challenged—for a super-smart woman, she could be amazingly dense—to being uninterested in him. His dad was welcoming when he made the rare trip to Iceland, but hadn't gone out of his way to make sure Ben spent time with him.

Neither of them had paid any attention to his progress at school and never expressed any interest when he stopped stuttering or guided him in any way, shape or form. He was expected to get on with it, so that's what he had done.

He'd become the person he was, confident and successful, all by himself. He had his mother's ruthless streak, he could also be uninterested and quickly grow bored of things that didn't hold his attention. He wasn't father material and he didn't have time to learn how to be one…

But Millie didn't want him to be a father, she didn't want him involved in his child's life at all. She wanted to raise the baby alone, with no input from anybody else. How would he be any different from a sperm donor?

And if he did get her pregnant, could he stay uninvolved? He liked control, having it and wielding it, so would he be able to stick to his promise to stay out of her, and his child's, life? His mother had never liked him, but she liked having power over him. His father had been fine with, or without, Ben's presence in his life. If he had a child, in whose footsteps would he follow?

Questions tumbled through his mind, just like those fluffy snowflakes tumbled through the night, and he couldn't find any answers. Could he keep his distance from Millie during the pregnancy and after the baby was born? Would he be able to carry on a relationship, even if it was business, and ignore her child…*his* child?

And what about his stuttering? He pushed his hands into his hair, irritated with his grasshopper thoughts.

His stuttering was, to an extent, hereditary—one of his uncles on his dad's side had a stutter, as did his grandfather. What if he passed his chronic stuttering on to his kid? How would Millie feel if he told her there was a chance her kid would inherit his speech impediment? Would she say *'thanks, but no thanks'*?

If she did that, and she most likely would, it would hurt like hell. His stuttering had caused him so much pain, but he'd overcome it. He'd made a few mistakes lately when speaking to Millie and those small lapses scared him to his soul. What was it about her that made him lose a smidgeon of his hard-fought-for control? He only stuttered when he got upset or was overly emotional.

He knew that having people in his life he cared about would lead to a resumption of his speech impediment. He'd proved that with Margrét and he'd promised himself he'd never go back to that deep, dark place where words stuck in his throat and his world closed in. To feel less than, stupid and unaccepted. No, he couldn't risk that, he'd worked too hard to go back to the place he was before.

He needed to run, to put as much distance between them as he could.

But then a tantalising thought dropped into his brain. What if he didn't?

What…what if he ran *to* her, had a fling with her and then let her go when their time was up? Millie was an outlier, an absolute temptation, and she pulled unwelcome feelings to the surface. He accepted that.

Normally, when he met a woman who interested him, who made him feel more, he never, after taking her to bed, followed up. He was terrified he'd feel something, *anything*, and was constantly on edge, waiting for his stutter to be triggered by even the smallest hint of emotion. He so was tired of being ruled by fear...

Oh, he had no intention of falling in love with Millie, being overcome by emotion—it wasn't an option. But Millie got to him quicker than most and he sensed lust and like, affection and joy flittering on the outer edges of his mind. They were softer, brighter, lovelier emotions and ones he refused to entertain. He knew his stutter walked in their shadow...

But what if he *managed to* control his feelings towards Millie? What if, instead of running away, instead of having brief encounters, he had a fling with Millie and spent concentrated time with her? What if he danced with his devils instead of running away from them?

If he could keep emotions under control with her, then he knew—*knew*—he'd have absolute control of *every* emotion going forward.

Absolute control over his feelings meant he'd never have to worry about his stutter again. He'd be free of it, free from its invisible but still strong chains. Free from the fear of its reappearance and he'd finally wash the stain on his soul away. He'd never be the boy who couldn't speak again.

It was an opportunity, one that wouldn't roll around again. And when he had his emotions under control, then he could decide whether or not to give her a child.

Millie walked down the stairs to the kitchen, dressed in a pair of jeans, a long jersey the colour of butter and knee-high, flat-soled boots. Because she'd spent most of the night looking out of the window, she knew it had stopped snowing around four and, by eight, the heavy clouds had lifted, allowing what little light there was to filter through the gaps in the clouds. With every hour that passed the day lightened. As much as a winter's day in Iceland could.

She wished she could say the same thing about her state of mind.

At the bottom of the stairs, Millie paused and placed her fist into the area between her ribs. She had to face Ben at some point and all she could do was apologise for the timing of her question. She couldn't, *wouldn't*, apologise for asking him to give her the baby she so desperately wanted.

But she hadn't approached the subject in the right way and for that she was sorry. She needed him to know she hadn't used sex as a means to butter him up, another thought that had occurred to her in the early hours. She hadn't, not even once, equated making love with having a baby...she only linked Ben and babies after they'd made love.

She'd wanted him. She'd wanted to know him in the most primal, biblical way a man and woman could know each other. She'd only considered the possibility of Ben as a donor after looking at the website and long after they'd had blindingly good sex. She wasn't, couldn't be, that manipulative. Did he understand that? If he didn't, she needed to convince him.

She wasn't good at heart-to-heart conversations,

at exposing herself emotionally or mentally. Since her mum's death and that blowout conversation with Magnús, she far preferred to keep people at a distance, that way they couldn't hurt or disappoint her.

But talk to Ben she would. She had to… But maybe she could do it later.

Ben's deep voice drifted over to her and stopped her flight up the stairs. 'Are you going to hover or are you going to come into the kitchen and have a cup of coffee?'

Right, *busted*. Millie wiped her damp hands on her jeans and pulled up a smile. Or tried to. She forced her feet to move, but when she saw him standing next to the island, looking down at his phone, all the air rushed from her lungs. Heat rocketed from her stomach to her womb and between her legs.

She wanted him again, desperately. She wanted to pull his navy sweater and white shirt up and over his head, tug that leather belt apart and drop his grey pants to the floor. Her hands itched to explore his chest, those lovely abs and his muscled back.

She wanted to fall into his kisses, and into the magic they'd found last night.

Ben looked up and their eyes connected. Heat flared in his eyes and his Adam's apple bobbed. Their physical attraction was undeniable, and she wished she could wipe the slate clean, go back to last night and start all over again.

Ben managed a small smile. 'Coffee?' he asked, putting his phone down on the counter.

'Morning. And, yes, please,' Millie slid on to a

bar stool and linked her hands together. Ben turned to the expensive coffee machine and Millie looked past his broad shoulders to the drifts of snow outside the window.

In the weak light, not dawn or daylight, his neighbourhood was now a pristine white landscape, as if Mother Nature had painted everything with a soft, fluffy brush. The trees lining the street were weighed down, their branches drooping under the weight of the snow. Icicles dropped from the eaves of the house over the road. 'Wow, that's a lot of snow,' she said, wincing at her inane statement.

'The main roads will be cleared in a few hours,' Ben explained, his back still to her. 'And they should open the airport soon.'

Right, he was hinting she should go back to London. She could do that. She *should* do that as soon as possible. But first, she had to apologise to Ben for making such a hash of things last night.

She pulled in some much-needed air and started to speak. 'I'm really sorry about last night, sorry I threw that at you and for the timing of my question. The thought popped into my brain and then left my mouth. I should've thought it through a bit more.'

Damn, she wished he'd turn around, she hated talking to his back. 'It's a huge ask. Also, I don't want you to think I only had sex with you because I was buttering you up to ask you to give me a baby. I don't operate like that, the one thing had nothing to do with the other and I only thought about you being a donor after I—'

Ben walked over to her and slid a cup of coffee in front of her. He gripped her shoulder. 'Breathe, Millie.'

'I will, in a minute, I just need you to understand—'

'Millie, take a breath and stop talking,' Ben commanded her.

Millie's mouth snapped shut. She looked at Ben and when she was reasonably sure he wasn't going to speak, she started talking again. 'I just need to say that I'm—'

'*Millicent.*'

Millie heard the exasperation in his voice and stopped talking. Her shoulders slumped and she dropped her head, letting her hair hide her hot face. She'd made such a hash of everything, and she felt like such a fool. She desperately wanted the floor to open up and swallow her whole. Millie felt Ben's hand skate over her hair and then burrowed under her hair to hold her neck in a gentle grip. 'Look at me.'

It took Millie twenty seconds, maybe more, before she mustered the courage to look at him. And when she did, she saw he was smiling and that his expression held no mockery and a hefty dose of compassion. 'Can you possibly keep quiet for a minute while I speak?' he asked and she heard the gentle teasing in the question.

She nodded. Well, she'd *try*.

'I didn't, for one minute, think that you were manipulating me last night. And I'm smart enough to recognise when I'm being used.' His grip on her neck tightened, just a fraction. 'I don't know you well, but you don't dissemble and you aren't manipulative.'

A whole lot of tension left her body and she sighed, relieved. Weight dropped off her shoulders, but she couldn't relax because he was going to shoot down her proposal. 'Thank you,' she murmured. 'I appreciate you saying that.'

Ben picked up her cup of black coffee and took a sip. 'I can see the question in your eyes, Millie. You still want an answer.'

She nodded. 'I do.' It was the truth after all.

Ben pushed an agitated hand through his hair, his mouth taut with tension. 'I can't give you one, I'm afraid. I know I should say no, but I can't. I can't say yes, either.'

'You need more time to think about it,' Millie said. She understood that and was perfectly happy to give him all the time he needed. Within reason. She wasn't going to hang around for ever waiting for an answer. She had a baby to make, a new life to start.

'I do,' Ben agreed.

Fair enough. 'That makes complete sense and I know I can't expect an immediate answer.' She'd like one, though. She thought about pushing him for a date, an end point and knew she was pushing her luck.

Rein it in, Piper. It's not as though you are asking to borrow some sugar or asking him to give you a lift to the airport.

'How long do you need?' she asked him.

He lifted his hands, puzzled. 'I don't know, Millie.'

She stared at her coffee cup, thinking hard. She'd been mentally prepared to delay getting pregnant until she and Ben were, at the minimum, legally separated. It would take them, at least, eighteen months to get their divorce through the system. Could she delay the baby-making process for half that time, say nine months, the same amount of time she required to grow a baby?

She wasn't crazy about the delay, but she was willing to wait if it meant there was a chance of having Ben's baby. She knew him, she trusted him and she wanted her child to carry his genes as well as hers.

'Do you think you could give me an answer in nine months?' Millie asked him.

She'd finally, finally, managed to crack his mask of imperturbability and shock, hot and blunt, flew through his eyes. 'You are prepared to wait *that* long?'

She lifted one shoulder. 'Yes. You are the only person I would consider entering into a nine-month baby deal.' She tried to smile, but knew she didn't succeed. 'My only request is what I've always asked of you, Ben, and that's for you to be honest. The moment you know whether you will, or won't, please tell me.'

He nodded, looking more serious than usual. 'I promise to tell you as soon as I can, Mils. And I promise to continue being honest with you.'

That's all she could ask. Right, time to move on from this awkward conversation. She was feeling like the one-night stand who'd overstayed her welcome and Ben had work to do. 'Can you check with Einar whether he managed to get me on a flight back to London?' she asked him. 'And do you think the bank will be open today?'

Ben nodded. 'I don't see why not. Why?'

'Well, I'd like to see what's in the bank deposit box Magnús rented in my name before I leave,' she told him, looking at the hands that had glided over her body last night. She wanted more of the wonderfulness they'd shared last night, but she couldn't ask him to take her back to bed. She torpedoed that option when she blurted out her baby-making idea.

Ben pushed his hip into the island and crossed his arms. He was so close she could count each of his individual, dark and stubby eyelashes and could see the faint, white scar on the right side of his jaw underneath his stubble. His big brain was working overtime and she wondered what he was thinking. She sighed. He was probably counting the minutes until he got the crazy woman out of his house.

'Why don't you stay?'

Millie blinked, unsure if her hearing was playing tricks on her. 'Sorry?' she asked.

'Stay,' he said. 'Here. With me.' Ben tapped his index finger against his bicep, the only hint he wasn't as insouciant as he sounded. 'I'm flying to St Barth's in two weeks, the afternoon before the gala concert—'

'I'm not happy about you missing the concert, Jónsson.' She narrowed her eyes at him, trying to channel Bettina. She also just wanted a minute to take in his words. Ben was asking her to stay. What did that, what *could* that, mean?

'I was hoping to talk you into the speech I've been asked to do,' she added.

'I'd rather die,' Ben growled and she wondered if he'd really turned white, or whether it was a trick of the light.

'You give speeches to hundreds, thousands of people all the time,' Millie countered. She'd caught a couple of his speeches on social media and she'd been impressed. Benedikt Jónsson, it was said, knew his stuff.

Ben's expression hardened. 'That's business, not personal. I don't *do* personal.'

His words were bullet hard and the hard light in his eyes suggested she not pursue this now.

'Spend the next two weeks with me,' he said, repeating his earlier suggestion. 'I'll take some downtime and I'll hand off some of my responsibilities to my second-in-command, and we can explore Iceland. It's been years since I've been snowshoeing or on a snowmobile.'

It had been even longer for her and she'd always loved Iceland best in winter. It had a stark beauty that took her breath away. Millie desperately wanted to reacquaint herself with this ancient, mystical land, and her first instinct was to shout yes, loudly and with force, but she managed to swallow her response.

'Why?' she asked instead. He couldn't do the speech for her, he didn't do personal, but he was asking her to stick around. She narrowed her eyes, suspicious. 'Why are you ditching work to spend time with me?'

Ben shrugged. 'Part of the reason is that I need to decide on whether to give you a baby and I think I need to know you better, and get to know you as an adult, to make that decision.'

His answer made sense, but it sounded… Millie bit the inside of her cheek. What was the word she was looking for? Rehearsed, maybe? Not a lie, but not the full truth either.

'And the other part?' Millie pressed him.

He scratched his neck, and his eyes slid off hers. 'You are like a human lie detector test. Look, I promised never to lie to you and I don't want to. Can I say that I am trying to work something out and leave it at that?'

She wanted to push, but sensed it wouldn't help. 'And you want me to stay in Reykjavik?' she clarified.

'Iceland is pretty special this time of the year and I thought it might be a good time for you to rediscover the country, as you've been away a long time.'

She had and she'd missed being here—she'd lost touch with her Icelandic roots. After their hasty marriage, she'd been desperate for a new life and a new place. It had taken her twelve years to return and she'd yet to lay all her ghosts to rest. Maybe if she spent some time here, she could work through the last of the resentment she held towards Magnús, she could remember her mum better and she could close the circle.

But there was another elephant in the room and this one was wearing very sexy lingerie. What about sex? Would Ben expect her to share his bed? Could they go back to where they were last night? She wanted to spend long, lovely hours in his arms, but was having a fling with him the clever thing to do?

But how was she supposed to *not* want to sleep with him? He was smart, interesting, gorgeous and had superior bedroom skills. And she *liked* him. She'd never liked any man as much as she did Ben.

Maybe she should forget everything—using him as a baby maker, exploring this land she once called her home, their explosive attraction—and go back to London and resume her life there, eventually forcing herself to make an uncomplicated choice from a sperm bank website. But she'd asked Ben to give her a baby. It wasn't a request she could take back.

Millie rubbed her hands over her face and, when she lowered them, she saw that Ben was looking at her, his eyes steady and warm. 'Stay here, spend some time with me and when it's time for you to go home I'll, hopefully, be able to give you an answer about giving you a baby.' His eyebrows pulled together in a frown. 'But I feel I should warn you that the chances of me saying yes are not high.'

'I told you, you don't have to do anything, be anything—'

Ben jammed his hands into the pockets of his pants and frustration flickered in his eyes. 'Millie, we went over it. I know what you said and I'll think it through, okay?' He looked at his watch and then picked his coffee off the counter. 'So, are you staying or are you going back to the UK?'

It was a choice between spending time with him or spending time in London, mostly alone. It was a choice between having his body wrapped around her when she slept, waking up to the smell of good coffee and a rumpled man in the morning and a series of great orgasms to…well, boredom. Loneliness.

Nobody, she decided, should be lonely at this time of the year. But before she agreed to stay here, she needed to know whether they were going to pick up where they left off. 'And are we going to keep sleeping together?'

Ben didn't drop his eyes from hers. 'Last night was amazing, but—'

Oh, dear, here came his *but*…

'Obviously I'd love to keep making love to you. But I don't want you to feel pressurised, that it's a condition of you staying. If we both want to, we can. If not, we remain friends.' He sent her one of those warm smiles that could melt her insides at fifty paces.

There was no point in trying to play it cool. 'I want to, Ben.'

A rare, full smile bloomed. 'Yeah, I do, too.'

'And are we friends, Ben?' Millie asked, tipping her head to the side.

'We're on our way,' Ben told her. It was a fair statement, but Ben knew her better than she knew him. 'Two weeks, Mils, let's go play. Let's forget about babies, work, divorce, the trust and what happens in the future and live in the moment. A two-week step out of time.'

Oh, that sounded like heaven. But the thought that life didn't work like that niggled at the back of her brain. They still had to be smart. 'Same terms as before?' she asked. 'No strings sex, complete honesty?'

He placed an open-mouthed kiss on her lips. 'That works. Can I get Einar to cancel your flights?'

Millie nodded quickly. 'Yes, please. Could you also ask him to see if he can get me an appointment at the bank so that I can deal with those safety deposit boxes?'

He nodded, scooped up his phone and in an instant he was talking to Einar, issuing a set of instructions in his machine-gun-fast Icelandic. Man, she had a long way to go before she became even mildly proficient in the language again. Thank goodness most Icelandic people spoke excellent English.

Millie slipped off the stool, but her progress to the coffee machine was halted by Ben's strong arm around her waist. While still talking to Einar, he deposited her back on the stool, but only on the edge and lifted her thigh to hold it over his hip. He smiled down at her as her core connected with his erection and she was pretty certain her eyes rolled back in her head. Because she wanted him to moan her name, she placed her hands on his hips and stretched out her fingers and allowed her thumbnail to scrape his long, hard length.

Ben was in the middle of a sentence about delaying some meeting—or she thought he was—but then his eyes darkened and he shuddered. He disconnected the phone mid-sentence and it clattered on to the surface of the island, coming to rest quite close to the far side. It buzzed with an incoming call, most likely Einar, but Ben ignored it and lowered his mouth to hers and slid his tongue past her teeth, to tangle with hers.

He jerked his head off her and stared down at her, his eyes blazing with need and passion. 'I'm taking you back to bed,' he told her in a deep growl. He lifted her and Millie wrapped her legs around his hips, loving his strength. Ben walked her up the stairs to the landing where he stopped to kiss her.

'I want you so damn much, Millie,' he told her, yanking her jersey up and over her head.

His need for her was obvious. It was in his touch, in the way he attacked her clothes, in his need to get her naked as soon as possible. She wanted him as much, as mindlessly, as completely.

CHAPTER SEVEN

Lying in the enormous bed in their exquisite room at a private, exclusive spa north of Reykjavik, Millie yawned and rested her head on Ben's shoulder after an extremely satisfying bout of lovemaking. She felt soft and floaty, a sorbet that had been left to melt under a hot summer sun. She pulled her knee up to rest it on Ben's thigh and felt the pull in her thigh muscles. *Ow.* Thank goodness she'd had a massage that afternoon—if she hadn't, she doubted she would still be able to walk.

She and Ben were a week into their Icelandic adventure and muscles she didn't know she possessed were saying 'hi'. Loudly and resentfully. Millie thought she was reasonably fit, but a week full of outdoor adventures—skiing, snowshoeing and ice skating—had her thinking that a few hours spent in the gym each week didn't amount to much.

They'd taken snowmobiles and explored Langjökull, the second-largest glacier in Iceland, but driving a snowmobile was so much harder than she remembered. But the experience had been amazing and sore muscles were a small price to pay to explore the amazing winter wonderland.

She'd forgotten how compelling and magical Iceland was, how endlessly beautiful. How effortlessly romantic.

'Have you ever been in love?' Millie asked, her voice breaking the comfortable silence.

He pulled back to frown at her. 'That's an out-of-the-blue question,' he stated. She shrugged. Did his body tense? Just a little?

'We're in a romantic room in a romantic place. I haven't, not really. I haven't experienced I-can't-live-without-you love,' Millie told him.

Ben stroked her head, then her shoulder. 'Have you enjoyed rediscovering Iceland?'

'So much,' she told him, kissing his chest, aware that he didn't answer her question. 'It's been brilliant.'

She'd always be grateful to Ben for joining her on her tour of rediscovering the land of her birth. Together, they'd marvelled at the Gullfoss waterfall, watched geysers shoot from the ground and walked through ice caves. And she'd never forget seeing a massive chunk of ice calving into the water and floating towards the sea at Jökulsárlón. Her Icelandic was, very slowly, improving and Ben, apart from taking and making a few phone calls, had left work behind.

Ben's phone lit up. He picked it up and squinted at the screen to read the message. Who was rude enough to send messages so late at night? Putting it back down on the bedside table, Ben turned his head to kiss her forehead and she expected a sleepy goodnight.

'Let's get up.'

She dragged her eyelids open and tipped her head back. It was shortly after midnight, what could he possibly want to do? 'Let me think about that…' she told him, yawning. '*No.* Go to sleep, you maniac.'

Instead of following what she thought was a very sensible suggestion, Ben left their bed and flipped the covers back. He slid one hand under her bum, the other under her back, and walked her to the en-suite bathroom. The huge shower was tucked into the corner and Ben placed her on her feet and flipped on the taps to the multi-headed shower.

'Can we not do this in the morning?' Millie asked as he handed her a band to keep her hair out of the pulsing spray.

Ben dropped a kiss on her nose. 'We could,' he agreed.

Millie's eyes widened as Ben stepped under the spray and quickly and efficiently washed. Shrugging at his hurried movements, she stepped under the lovely, hot spray and allowed the power shower to pummel her stiff shoulders. Mr Efficient could power his way through the shower, but she was in holiday mode and intended to enjoy every experience at this luxury geothermal spa. And that included spending many, many luxurious minutes enjoying this power shower.

She'd booked another spa appointment tomorrow and later they were taking a private tour to hunt for the Northern Lights. They could drive for hours, Ben warned her, and not see anything. Nature's most amazing light show only appeared when conditions were perfect—their appearance had something to do with solar activity, cloud cover and the darkness of the night sky. They might get lucky, or they might not.

Unlike Millie, who had been getting very lucky a *lot*.

Ben used a soapy flannel to wash her down and Millie's eyes flew open. 'I can wash myself, thanks,' she told him, irritated by his brisk strokes.

'Then can you hurry it up?' Ben asked, sounding uncharacteristically impatient.

What was his problem? If he wanted to get back to bed, he could leave her here to enjoy her shower in peace.

'You're killing me here, Mils,' Ben said, with a low groan. He dropped the flannel and used his hands to smooth soap across her body and Millie's protests died away. Her body, as it always did, melted under his skilled hands and she placed a hand on the wall to keep her balance when his hands moved between her thighs. She rocked against him, closing her eyes…he'd pulled more than a few orgasms from her earlier, yet here she was, on the edge again.

'Nope, not happening,' Ben muttered, shaking his head. 'Not right now.'

Millie looked down, saw he was interested and if they sat on the built-in ledge, they could add shower sex to their ever-increasing repertoire of sexual positions. Instead of stroking her, Ben yanked his hand from between her legs and pushed her under the shower so she could rinse the expensive shower gel from her body.

When she was free of soap, Ben turned off the shower and handed her one of the extraordinarily fluffy bathrobes hanging on a hook in easy reach of the shower door. He yanked his on and pulled her out of the bathroom.

Instead of leading her back to bed, he led her through the sliding doors on to the wooden deck outside and Millie yelped when her feet hit the icy planks. The cold air was a shock and she tried to turn around to rush back to the warmth of their bedroom, but Ben planted his feet and held her in place. 'Trust me, Millie.'

Millie hopped from foot to foot. 'Where are we going?' she demanded. 'And will you pay for my medical treatment when my toes drop off from frostbite?'

In the darkness, Ben's white teeth flashed as he smiled. 'The planks are nowhere near cold enough to give you frostbite, they are heated. Stop being dramatic and start walking. I promise it will be worth it.'

Millie glared at the back of his head as he led her down the wood deck path. Just a few yards away was a geothermal pool. Right, she remembered reading something about each room having its own pool. Yes, her toes were about to fall off, but having a midnight swim in a thermal pool was a perfect idea.

Then she remembered that it would be a skinny

dip and her swimming costume was back in her room. She tugged on Ben's hand. 'Ben, we can't swim naked,' she protested.

Ben stopped at the edge of their pool. Millie couldn't see any of the other pools now, only the wild north Atlantic as it crashed on to the rocks below them. 'Nobody can see us, and we can't see them,' Ben told her. 'Everyone else is asleep.'

He shrugged out of his dressing gown and Millie thought he'd never seen anything better than Ben standing on the side of the pool, tall and strong and utterly masculine. The night sky was clear, but so dark, and Millie thought it would be amazing to sit in the pool while fat snowflakes fell from the sky.

She heard the hiss of the geothermal spring and watched Ben slide into the water, his eyes closing in sensual delight. She saw a sign attached to the wall and moved to read it, barely able to make out the words in the dim light. It was a request that all the bathers shower before entering the pool. Right, that explained Ben bundling her into the shower.

'Come on in, Millie,' Ben told her.

Millie undid the sash, hung her robe alongside Ben's and tried not to feel embarrassed about being naked. It was no different from when they were in bed, she told herself. She darted a look at Ben and his look of appreciation imbued her with confidence. Using the steps, she slipped into the water...

And in five seconds, she died and went to heaven. The hot water was silky against her skin and her body heated instantly. She bent her knees and the water covered her shoulders. It was official: she might never leave this place.

Ben wrapped his arms around her waist and dropped a kiss on her temple. Millie looked up and took in the black velvet sky and the ice drop stars and felt completely happy, unbelievably content. Right now, right here, with this man, was where she most wanted to be.

'It's the most stunning night, cold but so clear,' Millie whispered, feeling the need to keep her voice down. It felt wrong to talk at normal volume when the air around them was so still.

'It is,' Ben agreed. He guided her to a ledge and sat, positioning her back to his front so they could look out to sea. He cupped one breast with one hand and laid the other on her thigh and Millie leaned her head back to rest her head on his collarbone. Hot water, an amazing sky and Ben. What else could she need?

'Bettina sent me the slideshow they are going to play at the concert, Ben, and a rough draft of the speech detailing her work with the foundation,' Millie lazily told him after they'd been silent for a few minutes. She could be quiet with Ben and she didn't feel the need to fill every minute talking.

'And?'

'It's good,' Millie said. 'Humorous and lovely without being maudlin. It'll be so hard to speak without crying, especially knowing you won't be there. I wish you'd change your plans and do the speech for me—'

'You need to do it, Millie,' Ben told her and Millie heard the *don't go there* note in his voice. A few days ago she'd asked him, again, whether he'd read the speech for her and got a curt, harsh 'no' as a reply.

'But I could delay my trip to St Barth's and fly out after the concert, if you *really* wanted me there.'

She tipped her head back and up so she could, sort of, look at his face. 'I *really* do want you there, Ben. And Jacqui loved you and I think your absence would be noticed.'

'I know,' he admitted, his voice sounding rough. 'It's j-just...' He hesitated for a few beats, before taking in a deep breath. 'I still miss her and I thought it would be easier to be somewhere else.'

Millie understood that. Being around people who loved her mum, and who wanted to talk about her, brought a lot of the pain of losing her back and it was a sharper stab than before.

'I'll change my plans, Mils, and I'll attend the gala concert with you. I'll fly out when it's done.'

'Thank you.' And maybe, somehow, she'd persuade him to do the speech for her. She sighed and tipped her eyes to inspect the bold, brash sky, filled with stars. 'This land... I'd forgotten how enchanting it is.'

She felt Ben drop a kiss into her hair—it was still in the messy bun she'd pulled it into before she went into the shower. 'It's nice to see you enjoying Iceland, Millie,' he murmured. 'The last time you were here, you couldn't wait to leave.'

True enough. She'd desperately wanted to get

away from Magnús and start a new life somewhere else. 'Iceland was too small for both of us,' she replied.

'You and me or you and Magnús?'

'My stepfather and I,' she clarified. 'Our relationship was nightmarish.'

Ben took a while to answer her. 'I now know that you had your problems after your mum died, but I thought that you two got along well before Jacqui died. Icelandic people don't get hung up about step kids and parentage. They're pretty welcoming. Why wasn't Magnús?'

'He resented me, resented the attention my mum gave me.'

'Why didn't Jacqui tell you about your biological father?'

It was a question she'd asked herself a thousand times. 'I don't know. She was unbelievably honest, yet she lied to me about Magnús until the day she died.'

Ben's chest lifted with his sigh. 'I've wondered about that, too, because Jacqui wasn't secretive.'

'Well, she kept one hell of a one from me,' Millie said, sounding bitter. 'And, yes, I'm still angry with her for leaving me with all these questions and what ifs.'

'What ifs?'

'I don't have a family, Ben…so what if my dad is out there and what if he needs a family as much as I do? What if I have an underlying medical condition that I have inherited from him? What if I pass

on something from him to any kids I might have?'
Behind her, Ben tensed. She was spoiling this night
by talking about her past and she should stop.

She sighed. She knew she was being overly dramatic. 'Not knowing who he is, whether he is still
alive or whether he even knew about me, keeps me
awake at night, Benedikt.'

He stroked her arm, from her shoulder to the tips
of her fingers. 'I know, sweetheart.'

'And it would help if I understood why my mum
kept it from me.' Millie half turned to face him. 'You
don't know anything about him, right?'

He looked her in the eye and pushed a strand of
damp hair off her forehead. 'No, sweetheart. I didn't
know anything about this until you told me.' Ben
cuddled her close. 'I'm so sorry, Millie. If it helps,
I wish I could go back in time—I'd change that for
you.'

Millie traced patterns on his wrist and up his arm.
'I just wished she'd trusted me,' Millie said. 'Between them, they did a good job of teaching me not
to trust anyone.'

'Explain that, Mils.'

'If my mum, the person who I loved, who loved
me, could lie to me, I think anybody can. And will.
But Magnús messed me up as well,' she added. 'I
hate the thought of being controlled and, because
he could never love me, I doubt anyone can, except,
maybe, any children I have. I wasn't a bad kid, Ben,
I tried so hard to be a good daughter, someone he
could love, but I never got there.'

'You do know it was his issue, Mils, and not yours?'

'Intellectually I do, emotionally, I still have my doubts. I've had guys who told me they loved me, but I could never quite believe it and, because I couldn't trust what they said, or them, they eventually gave up on me. Or I gave up on them.'

'Oh, Millie,' Ben murmured.

'I've spent so much emotional energy on trying to figure my mum and stepfather out, trying to work out their motives for doing what they did,' Millie told him, wiggling her toes. 'The only thing that gives me a little comfort is that I made Magnús's life hell for a few years. He took some hits for his daughter, the walking, talking PR disaster.'

'Yeah, you landed a few blows, Mils. Unfortunately, Magnús didn't take the heat, I did. You wouldn't believe how many times I had to sweet-talk a client, how many times I heard the "why should they give me their PR account when we couldn't manage to keep the founder's daughter out of the news cycle" question. I became an expert in tap dancing.'

Millie turned to face him and scrunched her face. 'Oh, Ben, I'm so sorry. I never imagined you'd take the flak for what I did.'

'I think I overcame the hurdle you presented, Mils,' he drily informed her.

Since he—they—now owned a multi-international firm with clients based all around the world, it was obvious he had.

Millie leaned her back against the bath's wall and

pulled her knees up to her chest. 'Thank you for marrying me, Ben. Thank you for giving me an out and for looking after my interests so well.'

'Why did you trust me enough to put yourself in my hands?' he asked, after a short, emotional silence.

She thought for a minute, wondering how to explain. 'I think it's because my mum did. And when I suggested that we get married, you didn't throw me out of your office, you listened to what I had to say. And you were so straightforward, so…blunt. I appreciated that. And I appreciated you writing down the terms of our marriage, what we could and couldn't do, what was expected.'

Ben picked up a curl that had fallen loose from her bun and rubbed the damp hair between his fingers. 'You do know our agreement couldn't be used in a court of law, right?'

Millie rolled her eyes at his question. 'Of course I do, Benedikt, I knew it back then, too. But that you wrote it down, with our signatures, meant something to me. I've always disliked shadows, but I felt back then, as I do now, that you are a man who stands in the sunshine. With you, I get what I see.'

She felt him tense and frowned when he pulled his shoulder and leg away from hers. What did she say? Why was he pulling back? Had she, in some way, got that statement, or him, wrong?

No, she was being ridiculous. Ben had been the same man for the past twelve years, nothing had changed. He was still as forthright and blunt as he ever was, as most Icelandic people, except for

Magnús, were. She was letting her imagination off its leash. But she had to ask. 'Is there something I should know, Ben? Something you aren't telling me?'

Ben dropped his head and brushed his lips across hers in a kiss that was both racy and reassuring. 'Sweetheart, you're getting worked up and that's not what I thought would happen at half-midnight in a hot pool.'

Right…he was *right*. But Millie noticed he didn't answer her question. She thought about asking him again, pushing for more, but suspected Ben would retreat behind his armour of implacability and reserve. No, she was being silly and was spoiling the moment.

Then Ben smiled, placed a hand on her shoulder and released an audible sigh. 'Finally,' he murmured. 'I was about to give up on you.'

Millie wondered who he was talking to, but, before she could ask him, he slipped off her seat and walked to the other side of the tub. Ben placed his forearms on the side of the tub and she copied his movements.

'What are we looking at, Ben?' she asked, noticing that his eyes were fixed on the horizon.

He lifted his hand and Millie looked to where he was pointing. She saw a hint of green and thought her eyes were playing tricks on her. Then the sky started to pulsate with the strangest, most beautiful luminous green light. Millie's mouth fell open and she clutched Ben's arm, digging her nails into his skin.

'Are those…could those be…am I looking at the Northern Lights?'

Ben gently removed her hand from his arm and pulled her to stand in front of him and bent his knees so that their bodies were immersed in the water.

'I received a text alert when we were in bed saying that the conditions were optimal and that there was a good chance of them making an appearance. I didn't tell you because I didn't want you to be disappointed if they didn't appear.' He rested his chin on the top of her head as yellow joined green in a slinky, sensuous tango across the sky. 'I was about to call it a night and take you back to bed when I saw a hint of green on the horizon.'

Millie nodded, unable to speak as more of the celestial dancers took to the sky. Pink waltzed with blue, orange with purple in an indescribable light show. It felt as though some mystical force in the universe was finger painting, drawing an omnipotent finger through a palette of brightly coloured oil paints.

Millie stood in Ben's arms, utterly transfixed. It seemed to her that the world was holding its breath and the sea had stopped throwing waves against the rocks in deference to the majesty of the lights. She didn't want to talk or examine how she was feeling— her thoughts and emotions and her entire existence were all inconsequential right now. She was glad that Ben seemed to understand that words would spoil the moment.

He just held her, occasionally drifting a finger across her skin under the water to remind her he was there, here with her. Millie forgot her face was cold, that the night seemed darker than it had been before. All she could do was to try, in the best way she could, to take it all in.

She wanted to make memories and wanted every hue, every wave, every drumbeat of colour to be burned on her internal memory bank. She knew she was privileged to witness this, to stand under a majestic sky and be both overwhelmed and en-tertained. She couldn't tell how long they watched the lights, it could've been minutes or days, but she didn't care. Although he'd witnessed the ultimate light show many times before, Ben didn't rush her, he just waited until the last flicker of colour faded away before leading her out of the pool. Bemused, and bewitched, Millie kept looking at the sky as he shoved her into her gown, before pulling on his own. It was only when he guided her on to the icy wooden path that led back to their suite that she was shocked back into reality.

'I can't believe that happened,' she whispered. His hand tightened around hers and she felt rather than saw his contented smile.

'It was one of the more intense ones I've seen,' Ben admitted, his deep voice sliding over her skin like melted molasses.

She tugged on his hand and braked. Ben stopped and turned around. When he lifted his eyebrows, she cleared her throat and tried to speak past the emo-tion. 'Thank you. That was…um…unbelievable. I will never forget…' She dashed her tears away with impatient fingers.

Seeming to understand she couldn't express what she wanted to say, how emotional she felt, Ben dropped his head to kiss her temple. 'Let's go to bed, sweetheart.'

CHAPTER EIGHT

MILLIE THOUGHT THAT after a good sleep her revving-in-the-red-zone emotions would die down. But the next morning, watching Ben—dressed only in jeans and a cashmere sweater over a long-sleeved shirt—talk on his mobile outside, she knew everything had changed.

She wanted Ben in her life. Permanently. She wanted him as a lover, a husband and the father of her children. But loving someone meant trusting them, something she found intensely hard to do. She couldn't handle Ben lying to her, couldn't cope if he disappointed her. He could hurt her and cut her into a million emotional pieces.

But, despite their amazing Icelandic fling, him showing her the country of her birth, the laughter and the loving, she knew he hadn't caught as many feelings as her. Or any at all.

She was his wife, but in name only. He was her lover, but he'd given her no hint he wanted to continue seeing her after the gala concert, and they hadn't spoken again about her sperm donor request.

Despite them spending every moment of the last ten days together, she didn't know him much better than she had when she first arrived in Reykjavik. It was obvious there was so much below his urbane façade and she couldn't access any of his hidden depths. Millie didn't know if she ever would. Ben was an island, a place you got to visit, but never to know.

It was so typical of her that the one man she loved, the only person she'd ever fully trusted, was the one man who only wanted a specific amount from her and no more. He knew so much about her, far more than anyone else, yet what she knew about his inner world would fit on a postage stamp.

Something was bugging him, he was wrestling with an issue. What was he trying to work out? Why couldn't he share it with her? Why did he need to hide it? Why wouldn't he let her help? She wanted to be the person he confided in, the woman who knew him better than anyone else. The one he turned to, valued, whose opinion was important.

Millie placed her hand on the cold glass and sighed. Ben's back was to her, and she took in his height, his strength, his solidity. Was she imagining herself to be in love with him because he was exactly what she wanted in a man? As a father for her children? Oh, he wasn't perfect, far from it. He could be impatient and unbelievably, tactlessly blunt, but he was, at the core of him, solid and calm. But so emotionally elusive...

Ben turned, saw her looking at him through the

window and his slow smile heated her from the inside out. He dropped his phone to his side and walked over to the door, sliding it open. Millie stepped back and squealed when he put his cold hand on her cheek.

'How can you be out there without a jacket?' she asked.

'Viking blood,' he quickly replied. 'It's a couple of degrees warmer than it was yesterday.'

Millie shook her head. 'That doesn't help when the temps dip below zero, Jónsson.' She saw that the light was fading and shook her head. It wasn't even three in the afternoon yet!

Ben tossed his phone on the coffee table that stood between the two couches and perched on the arm of the nearest couch. 'I was just talking to Einar about rearranging my St Barth trip. I'll be missing the first night of my friend's stag do, but that's not an issue.'

Millie winced. 'Look, if you need to be there—'

'All I'll miss is the hangover the next morning,' Ben assured her. 'Einar also spoke to Bettina who is, supposedly, delighted I will be escorting you. It's good PR,' he said, humour dancing in his deep blue eyes.

'Jacq's daughter and ex-partner arriving together will make a good story and will generate headlines and good press for the foundation.'

Was that why he had agreed to accompany her to the gala concert? Because it would be excellent PR for the Star Shine Foundation? Did his change of heart have anything at all to do with her? She thought he'd agreed to be there to support her, but now she wasn't so sure.

'Imagine the headlines if they knew we were married,' Millie said. 'There would be a firestorm of press attention.'

Ben pulled a face. 'I manage people who find themselves the target of a camera lens, not the other way around. Extricating celebrities from their self-created dramas is, *was*, the least favourite part of my job.'

Millie laughed. For a guy who ran an international PR firm, he should show more enthusiasm for celebrities and their need for good PR than he did, she told him. 'How on earth did you handle the PR for Daft Peanut and Gladys?' she asked.

She'd caused a few headlines in her day, but the antics of the young, over-the-top DJ who'd burst on to the music scene ten years ago and the bad girl of Scandinavian music were enough to turn any PR person grey.

'I tore my hair out with both of them,' Ben told her. 'The greatest day of my life was when I handed the clients over to my subordinates. I was finally able to run the business without having to stop to deal with their drama. Then, as soon as I could, I diversified and appointed an excellent manager to handle the high-value, high-drama clients. As you, as part-owner of the business, should know.' The comment was pointed and showed Millie that her lack of interest in their jointly owned business frustrated him.

'I have just enough interest in business practices

to run my small operation, Ben. PR Reliance was my mum's baby, not mine,' she told him. She pointed a finger at him. 'And, be honest, you would hate having an involved, interested partner. It suits you just fine for me to be a silent partner.'

Ben placed his empty cup on the coffee table and folded his arms. 'Maybe,' he conceded.

'Maybe my foot,' Millie retorted.

Ben tapped his index finger against his bicep. 'We were talking about the gala concert,' he said, changing the subject because he knew she was right. 'Because of you, I have to smile at the cameras and people, and shake many, many hands and kiss many, many cheeks.' Ben pulled a face. 'And I'll have to wear a tuxedo, which I hate.'

'Poor baby,' Millie gently mocked him. 'At least you don't have to do a speech honouring your dead mum.'

'*Touché.* You've definitely got the tougher gig,' he softly said. He ran his hand down her hair. 'You'll be fine, Mils.'

'You'd be finer,' she whipped back.

'Give it up, Mils, I'm not doing your speech for you,' Ben wearily stated, gripping the bridge of his nose.

She didn't want an argument with him, so she rested her temple against his bicep and wound her arms around his waist. He gathered her close and placed his chin on the top of her head. 'Didn't you say that you had booked a spa treatment some time soon?' he asked.

She had. 'Mmm. At three-thirty.'

'It's half two, now,' Ben told her, stepping back from her. She caught his mischievous smile as he gripped her hand in his and led her to the bedroom. 'That means I have forty-five minutes. Between sex and your spa treatment, you're going to need a nap later.'

Millie tried, but couldn't find any problems with his statement.

Ben took her empty takeaway cup and asked her if she wanted another hot chocolate. Millie debated for a minute—of course she did, they were delicious!—and it took all of her willpower to shake her head. 'I'd better not,' she told him, 'or else there is no way I'm going to fit into my dress for the gala concert.'

She thought of the gold, tight-fitting jersey top and the lighter gold flowing skirt she'd bought yesterday, after seeing it in the window of a small boutique on Laugavegur Street. While she didn't think that one hot chocolate would cause her to put on weight, the pastries she was addicted to, and the other delicious Christmas foods Ben kept insisting she try, would add to her waistline.

At this rate, she might not fit into her plane seat when she flew back after New Year. Ben threw their cups into a rubbish bin as Millie took in the square. The market at Jólaþorpið was fifteen minutes from Reykjavik. It echoed the beauty of the town of Hafnarfjörður and was a typical Christmas market.

Twinkling fairy lights criss-crossed the space

between the booths and jaunty instrumental music floated through the air. Millie had picked up a few Christmas gifts from stalls selling homemade jams and jewellery, Christmas decorations and woollen products. And there was food...so much food.

The long hours of dusk, that magical light, made the market extra festive, but it was cold and Millie stamped her feet, trying to get her blood flowing.

'Cold?' Ben asked, running his bare fingers down her cheek.

Since her nose was probably red, she couldn't lie. 'I am. But I'll be fine once we start moving.'

Ben curved his hand around the back of her neck and his warm lips met hers. 'Then let's walk. Do you want to try to find the Huldufólk?'

The Huldufólk, or hidden people, were elves in Icelandic folklore and were said to be supernatural creatures living in the wild. They looked and acted like humans and could make themselves visible at will. So it was said.

Millie squinted at him. 'C'mon, Ben, you don't really believe in them, do you?'

He shrugged. 'I don't *not* believe in them. It's part of the Icelandic tradition and culture and every culture needs a little magic.'

Millie remembered talk about the hidden folk from when she was little. 'I always thought your house had Huldufólk living in your garden,' she admitted. 'I loved visiting your dad, I would spend hours in the garden hoping I'd see one.'

Ben took her gloved hand in his. 'Well, Hellisgerdi Park is not far from here and they say it's the home of many Huldufólk. It's also a pretty walk and decorated for Christmas. Want to see it?'

Millie nodded, feeling the heat of his bare hand through the wool. He radiated warmth and she immediately felt warmer as they headed for the park. As they approached the park, whispers of déjà vu fluttered inside her and she was certain she'd visited here with her mum when she was very small. Candy canes and twinkling Christmas lights provided light to the cleared path, but snow covered the ground, small hills and the branches of trees.

'I think I only ever came here in summer,' Millie told Ben. 'It looks like an enchanted garden, doesn't it?'

He nodded. 'There are lots of lava formations that are blanketed in moss, so it's easy to convince kids, and adults, that elves live here. My dad insisted the hidden folk were real.'

Millie looked up at him, surprised. 'I think that's the first time you've ever mentioned your dad,' she said. 'You don't talk much about your family.'

He looked away. 'You know the basics, English mother, Icelandic father. I went to boarding school in the UK. I spent a couple of school holidays with him.'

'No siblings?'

'No.' So they were both only children of only children. And Millie knew it was a lonely way to grow up.

She'd like to know much more than the basics

of his past. And because he opened the door, she strolled on through. 'What was he like?'

'Stoic and direct, a big believer in the Icelandic philosophy of *þetta reddast*.'

'Everything will work out,' Millie murmured.

Ben rocked his hand from side to side. 'Sort of, but not quite,' he replied. 'It's less starry-eyed optimism and more the idea that you sometimes have to make the best of things, just work through it.' He gestured to the banks of snow.

'Take the recent blizzard for example. It's not the first, it won't be the last and it wasn't nearly the worst the country has seen. We've got volcanoes and glaciers and we have to live in this hostile environment and make it work for us. We accept that sometimes life does work out and sometimes it doesn't, but you have to try.'

'And that's how you built up PR Reliance,' Millie said. 'But you took it from a small national concern to an international empire.'

'That's my English mother's bull-headed determination. If you tell me I can't do something, then I will.'

'Are you more English than Icelandic?' Millie asked him, intrigued.

Ben looked down at her. 'What do you think?'

She took some time to sort through her thoughts, before answering him. 'You are very blunt, so you are Icelandic in that. You're punctual, that's English because Icelandic people are not. I know that you are a huge believer in equality and that's very Icelandic.

But I think you are very English in your outlook on relationships.'

He stopped walking to look down at her. 'What do you mean by that?'

'Well, I want a baby, as you know.'

'You might've mentioned it once or twice,' Ben replied, a little drily.

She narrowed her eyes to fake-scowl at him. 'Anyway... Iceland has one of the highest birth rates in Europe and there are young women everywhere with babies and who are pregnant. Some are in relationships, some aren't. But Icelanders have this idea that babies are always welcome and there isn't angst around blended families. Yet you are—' She hesitated, unsure of how to put this into words.

'I'm what?' he prompted her.

'I think the English part of you is hesitating—if you were fully Icelandic, I'd probably be pregnant by now.'

'I appreciate your confidence in my baby-making skills,' Ben murmured.

But he didn't contradict her and that was interesting. 'So you don't subscribe to the-more-the-merrier idea of kids? Or *þetta reddast* when it comes to having kids?'

He took her hand, tucked it into his elbow and they started walking again. 'No, I don't.'

Right, don't overwhelm me with information, Jónsson.

Millie started to tell him he didn't need to be involved in the raising of the baby, but held her words back. Two weeks ago, she thought she wanted to be a single mum, but now she wasn't sure. She now wanted more from Ben, as a lover and as a father.

'It's unlike you not to take the opportunity to try to convince me to give you a child, Mils,' Ben commented.

She scrunched up her nose and hoped he didn't notice. She wasn't sure what to say—her heart wanted to beg him to love her, to create a family with her, and to plan a life together—but she knew he would run a mile if she suggested any of the above. Ben didn't do commitment, he'd told her that. More than once. And at some point, she had to let that sink in, take it onboard.

'What was your mum like, Ben?' she asked instead. Maybe if he understood more about his past, she would understand him a bit better.

He sighed. 'Driven, cold, emotionally stunted.'

Wow, okay then.

'She was a nuclear engineer, right?'

'Yes, she worked for a company I'm pretty sure is a cover for the British government,' Ben told her. 'She was obsessed with her work and I got my work ethic from her.'

'And, possibly, your dad. People in Iceland aren't slouches when it comes to working.'

'Point taken, but my mother was a next-level workaholic. Nothing ever came between her and her work,' he said and Millie heard a note of…something in his voice. Longing or resentment—a combination of both? She wasn't sure.

'Tell me something good about her,' Millie said, wanting him to move on to a happier memory. It was what she did, or what she was trying to do, when she got caught up in the *Why didn't my mum believe me or be honest with me?* spiral. 'Did she binge eat chocolate or have a funny laugh?'

She'd never met his mum and she wondered about the woman who'd birthed him. She felt Ben pull away from her, just a little, and she followed, tucking herself back into his side. She wasn't going to allow him to scoot away, emotionally or physically.

'She was super-intelligent, her IQ was off the charts,' Ben eventually told her. 'She would never mix her food—if she had potatoes, vegetables and meat on her plate, she'd eat each one separately. Ah, what else? She was utterly unemotional, brutally honest and had no concept of tact. If she thought you were an idiot, then that's what you were. She believed you could do anything you wanted to, achieve anything at all, as long as you put your mind to it and worked hard. She didn't accept failure, ever.'

Millie rubbed her cold and itchy nose with the side of her hand. She knew, from those few sentences, that she hadn't been fun to live with and her expectations of Ben had been off the charts. Being raised by somebody like that had to have been difficult. No wonder he wasn't a warm and fuzzy type of guy.

'Is she the reason you don't want to have kids?' Millie asked. 'Because you suspect you might be like her?'

Ben stopped and looked down at her. In the half-daylight, half-night light, his eyes were a hard blue. 'I'm exactly like her, Millie, don't think I'm not.'

She laughed and Ben jerked back. 'Don't be ridiculous, you're nothing like that! Sure, you don't wear your heart on your sleeve, but you know how to laugh and you know how to make a woman feel special. You've listened to me talk about my mum and my issues with Magnús. You helped me re-balance those scales. You took me all over the country on a holiday trip I'll never forget and were thoughtful enough to hang around in a hot pool, hoping for the lights to appear because you knew how much I wanted to see them. You *see* me, Ben.'

'You don't know me, Millie, not really,' Ben told her.

He looked so serious and Millie felt a frisson of fear run up her spine. 'Of course I do,' she protested. 'Okay, maybe I don't know all your history, but I know what makes you *you*. You embody what I value most…'

'And that is?' he challenged.

'Honesty,' she told him. 'You've always been honest with me and that means more to me than anything else.'

Ben released a tiny snort, part-laughter, part-derision. 'You're seeing me through rose-coloured glasses, Millie.'

'Are you telling me that you haven't been honest with me?' Millie demanded.

'I'm telling you that you've chosen to see what

you want to see. You still think that I'm going to cave and give you a baby, don't you?'

How had a massive chasm opened up between them, why were they suddenly arguing? Millie saw the annoyance in Ben's eyes and, when he repeated his question, she threw her hands up in the air. 'I'm hoping that you are,' she admitted. She was also hoping he'd come to love her and that they'd have a life together.

'Please don't bank on it, Millie.'

CHAPTER NINE

BACK IN REYKJAVIK, Millie left the taxi and walked up the path to Ben's front door. She slipped inside his house, kicked off her boots in the hall and hung her coat up on a rack. She rested the package on the hall table, still unable to believe the contents held within the plain cardboard box.

Finally alone, she slid down the wall to sit on the cold floor of the hallway and tears, hot and acidic, slid down her cheeks. The house had underfloor heating, but the hall, separated from the rest of the house by frosted glass doors, was chillier.

She just needed a moment to get herself under control, a few minutes to make sense of what was in the box. She'd wanted answers, but they weren't what she'd expected. Not even close.

Millie heard the glass doors opening, but she didn't look up, silently begging Ben to go away. She didn't want to explain the reason for her tears, wasn't sure if she could. There were no words…

Not for what she'd just discovered.

Millie felt Ben's hand on her head and then he

crouched down in front of her, easily balancing on the balls of his feet. He placed his finger under her chin and lifted her face, but Millie slammed her eyes shut, not wanting him to see her cry.

'Ah, sweetheart, what's got you in such a state?' Ben asked, placing both his hands on her bent knees.

She darted a look at the brown box. 'I went to the bank,' she told him.

'Okay,' Ben said. 'You can tell me all about it, but we need to get you up off this cold floor first.'

He stood, gripped her hands and pulled her up. Cupping her face, he used his thumbs to brush away the tears before holding her head against his chest. Millie buried her nose into that space where his shoulder met his neck, inhaling his sea-and-sunshine scented cologne, her arms around his waist. Ben held her close and Millie knew he'd hold her until she was ready to talk, to make the next move, or leave his arms.

She could stay here for ever, he gave the best hugs, but she knew she had to face down the contents of that box. She couldn't avoid it or ignore it, she couldn't choose only the best parts of her past.

'I didn't expect you to be here,' she told Ben.

'Nothing needed my attention at the office. I was missing you, so I came home,' Ben told her.

Millie stepped back and bent her knees to pick up the box, but Ben got there first, lifted it and tucked it under his arm. He opened the glass door leading into the open-plan lounge, dining and kitchen area and placed the box on the wooden table in the kitchen area. He suggested that Millie sit and asked her if she wanted some wine.

She glanced at the oversized clock on the cherry-red wall above the stove. It was only three in the afternoon and a bit early.

'I'm done with work for the day and you're on holiday, so why not?' Ben asked.

Why not indeed? Millie watched as he chose a bottle of wine from the rack next to the fridge, remembering he had a state-of-the-art cellar in the basement. It was next to the state-of-the-art gym and the sauna, which was also top of the range.

Millie took the huge glass Ben held out to her and sipped. Ben slid on to the bench across the table from her, waiting for her to tell him the reason for her tears.

If she didn't tell him, if she changed the subject and moved on, he would let her. Ben didn't push. Millie took another sip of her wine and stood, moving to stand at the head of the table. She lifted the lid on the box and looked at Ben.

'As you know, I went to the bank to find out what Magnús put in the safety deposit box. And it was Magnús, he paid to rent it and I'm the only person who can access it. I have no idea why he didn't send the contents to me, directly.'

'I suppose there are no gold bars, loose diamonds or wads of cash?' Ben asked.

She shook her head. 'No, nothing like that.' She picked up the top file, saw that it was labelled with her mum's name and rested it on the table between the box and Ben. 'These are some of my mum's papers, her birth and death certificate, her schooling records, letters between her and her parents. I never thought to ask where they were, I assumed you had them.' She picked up a picture, smiled at the two stick-like figures and handed it to Ben.

He studied her childish drawing and the side of his mouth lifted in a sexy smile. 'I see your sketching skills hadn't yet kicked in,' he commented.

'I was four,' Millie protested. She pointed to the purple bobs around her mother's neck and at her ears. 'I did draw her necklace and earrings, though.'

Ben chuckled and handed the drawing back. She looked at it again, saw her wonky handwriting, Millie and Mum, and thought she might frame it and put it in her baby's nursery. Dipping her hand into the box, she pulled out a thick file. It was unlabelled and she handed it to Ben.

He frowned, placed it on the table in front of him and flipped open the cover. His expression became more puzzled as he flipped through the papers. 'These are prison records, Mils.'

She sat on the bench next to him and Ben shuffled over to give her more room, but kept his strong thigh against hers, giving her the anchor she so badly needed. 'Yeah, he was in and out of jail for most of his life. Icelandic jails, Danish jails—he even did a stretch in the UK.'

Ben picked up a photograph of a narrow-faced man with dark hair and winged eyebrows. He looked from her to the photo and back again. 'This is your dad,' he quietly stated. 'You have his nose, his eyes, his eyebrows, the line of your jaw.'

Millie nodded. 'Yep.'

She tapped her index finger on the photograph between them. 'His name is Hans Grunsmar, his mother was Icelandic and his father Finnish, according to his birth certificate. He was thirty-eight when he died and thirty when I was born. He was in jail at the time.'

'Wow.'

Millie thought she might as well tell Ben the rest. Or as much as she'd gathered from skimming the police records and letters her mum and parents exchanged. 'He and my mum were never married and they met when she was young, eighteen or nineteen. He was ten years older than her and he was married. Her parents freaked at their relationship and banned my mum from seeing him. So they ran away together, to Manchester.'

Millie blinked back her tears, thinking of the letters her mum wrote to her parents and never sent.

'He was abusive, emotionally and physically. He made my mum believe her parents didn't love her any more and wouldn't take her back, that they were ashamed of her. As a result, she spent far longer with him than she should've.'

Ben's big hand came to rest on her back and his rhythmic strokes calmed her down.

'Tell me what you found out, Mils,' he softly commanded.

'She fell pregnant with me and when she was six

months pregnant, he put her in hospital with a broken jaw.'

Ben released an angry growl and Millie rested her temple on his shoulder. 'That's not the worst of it, Ben.'

'There's more?'

Unfortunately. 'While she was in the hospital, she found the courage to call her parents. They dropped everything to go to her. They'd tried to contact her, but he monitored her mobile and deleted their calls, emails and messages. Anyway, with them in her corner, she laid charges against him. Mum told them she had hidden photos showing the other beatings he gave her. When the police searched his stuff, and their flat, they got more than they bargained for.'

Ben tensed.

'They found evidence linking him to sexual assaults and burglaries. He'd attacked many women over many years. The man was awful.'

Ben released a soft curse. 'Did your mum go back to live with her parents?'

Millie nodded. 'Yes, she lived with them until I was born, and afterwards. But when I was six months old, they were killed in a car crash. That's when she moved to Iceland.'

Ben's hand curled around her waist as he flipped the folder closed. 'That's awful, Millie. I'm so sorry.'

'You know, I've been so worried about what bad genes my baby will inherit from an anonymous donor, but now I'm worried about what genes he might inherit from my father!' she said, sounding a little unhinged.

'I believe nurture will trump nature, Mils. None of your bio father's genes came out in you and they won't come out in your kid.'

He sounded so certain and she wanted, desperately, to believe him. 'Are you sure, Ben?'

'Jacqui was an amazing mum, Mils, and you will be, too,' Ben told her, without a hint of worry in his voice. He closed the files and stacked them. His complete certainty calmed her fears. 'I'm so sorry that happened to her.'

'Me, too. She had such a hard time,' Millie stated. 'But now I understand why she kept my real father a secret and why she pretended Magnús was my dad.'

'She was trying to protect you from the knowledge that your father was a serial rapist.'

Millie turned to face him and put her elbow on the table. 'I think it would've been a lot better and healthier for me if she just told me that my dad was a bad man and left it at that. Thinking Magnús was my dad, but knowing he didn't love me, did some damage, Ben.'

He ran his hand over her hair. 'I know, Mils.' He pulled her in for a long side-to-side hug before pushing her heavy, long fringe off her face. 'I'm going to try to say this as gently as I can...your childhood is over, Millie. You've got to let it go. You can't keep carrying that baggage around with you.'

She nodded, tears streaming down her face. 'I *know*. I do know that, Ben, I just don't know how to put it down, to walk away from it. Tell me how to do it and I will,' she gasped the words out, her chest heaving with the concentrated emotion of a lifetime. 'Tell me how not to be angry and hurt and devastated and I will change, I will be better, I promise you!'

Ben pulled her into the shelter of his big body and wrapped his arms around her, holding her tight. 'Ah, Mils. Just be you. You are more than enough. You always were and always will be.'

She sobbed and held on to his words.

As the limousine made its way through the still snowy streets of Reykjavik, Millie smoothed down her golden skirt and touched her hair, pinned up into a romantic wavy bun on the back of her head. The loose style was supposed to look, as her stylist said, as if she'd just rolled out of bed, but it had taken hours for her to do.

Ben took her hand in his and squeezed it. 'You look wonderful, Millie.'

'For the daughter of a criminal, you mean,' Millie snapped back. She closed her eyes, immediately remorseful. She'd had a long, tough day and was still coming to terms with the contents of the safety deposit box. 'Sorry, I didn't mean that. I'm just on edge and tense and so nervous about making this speech.'

Ben gave her a reassuring smile. 'If I'd had any idea what you were going to find in the safety deposit box, I would never have asked the bank manager to see you on the same day as the concert.'

He'd pulled some strings to get her the appointment and she was grateful.

'It's not your fault, Benedikt,' Millie told him. Man, he looked amazing. He wore a classic tuxedo, but instead of a bowtie, he wore a plain black silk tie. He looked stunningly handsome and very debonair. She wondered what the press would think about them arriving together in the same limousine, then remembered the world knew them to be business partners.

In the eyes of the world, they were the two people closest to Jacqui and there was nothing to be read into them attending the gala concert together.

'It's not your fault either, Millie,' Ben told her, his tone suggesting she not argue with him.

She nodded. She took his hand and slid her fingers between his, grateful he'd lifted the privacy screen in the limo and that the windows were so darkly tinted that no one could see inside. She looked at Ben and managed a smile.

'I know, Ben. And I do understand why Jacqs didn't want me to know about him, he wasn't a very nice man. No, he was an awful man, but I'm choosing to believe I inherited all my genes from my mum, she made me the person I'm today.'

'She did,' Ben agreed.

'And I can see why she thought Magnús would be a good dad for me, he was handsome and educated, cool and controlled. He was everything my biological father wasn't. When she married him, she couldn't see into the future, she didn't know he couldn't love me. In fact, I don't think she ever admitted to herself that Magnús didn't love me. She always had an excuse for why he wasn't affectionate or loving or interested.' Millie folded the fabric of her dress into creases. 'It was as though she was trying to convince herself as much as me.'

'Stop fiddling with your gown,' Ben gently told her.

She sighed and smoothed the fabric back into place. 'I understand why she chose not to tell me—if I was faced with the same choice of protecting my little girl, maybe I would make the same decision. She kept the secret because she believed not knowing was best for me.'

'I agree. You were her whole world, and she would've fought dragons for you.'

It was true, her mum loved her more than life itself and Millie could understand, possibly even forgive her actions. And since it was the only misstep Jacqs ever made as a mother—for all of her life she'd been the awesome mum most girls dreamed of—she could stand up on that stage in front of two thousand people, Europe's princes and princesses, CEOs and celebrities, and talk about her mum. Well, theoretically.

In reality, she was terrified of messing up and making a hash of her mum's tribute speech. Her stomach lurched up into her throat. She hadn't done any public speaking, ever, and now she was going to talk in front of two thousand people the day she'd discovered who her real father was.

In the reflection on the window opposite, she saw

her bone-white face. Yep, terrified. 'I don't know if I can do this, Ben.'

Ben's smile was warm and reassuring. 'Of course you can, Millie.'

'Can't you do it for me?' she demanded. 'I might freeze or stumble or mess it up.'

'You'll regret not doing this later, Millicent,' Ben told her, moving towards her to drop a kiss on her temple. 'You *must* do this, for her.'

She really didn't think she could and told Ben so.

'You'll have a teleprompter in front of you and two on each side of you. You just have to read the words on the screen, words you helped write, Millie. The speech is great and you've practised it many times.'

After her fifth rehearsal, Ben, who had something of a photographic memory, could correct her without referring to the printed page. It was most annoying.

'You can imagine the audience naked if it helps, Mils,' Ben told her, sitting back. He reached for the glass of champagne he'd poured earlier, an exceptional Taittinger, and forced it into her hand. 'And drink this.'

She pushed the glass away. 'I should keep my head clear.'

He pushed the glass into her hand. 'One is fine, two or three would be a disaster.'

'Is that what you do, Ben, when you do your presentations?' she asked after the lovely liquid streamed down her throat. 'Drink champagne and imagine your audience naked?'

Ben snorted. 'The image of my colleagues naked is one I'd prefer not to have in my head.'

Millie laughed. 'So how do you do your big speeches?' she asked. 'You've spoken to far bigger audiences than I will tonight.'

'Mine are business speeches, Millie, very dry and boring. And longer,' Ben said, throwing his champagne back. 'Yours will be shorter and lovelier and you'll be talking about someone you love.'

Millie nodded and blinked back her tears. She rested her head against the window and closed her eyes. Ben was flying out after the concert to St Barth's for a friend's stag weekend and she was booked on tomorrow's afternoon flight back to London.

Theoretically, they were done, whatever they had was over. Neither of them mentioned their affair continuing after tonight and Millie didn't know when, if, she'd ever see him again. How could anyone expect her to walk away from him? How could this just *end*? And why hadn't they spoken about this? Had she hoped that by ignoring it, it wouldn't happen?

'I don't want you to go,' she told him. She kept her eyes closed. 'I don't want this to end.'

'We said two weeks, Mils,' he murmured.

She recalled every word they had exchanged, so she didn't need him reminding her of their deal. 'No strings, keep it simple, don't complicate the issue,' she muttered.

'Millie, this isn't the time to discuss this.'

She forced herself to look at him. 'Will there ever be *a* time?' she asked him, needing to know.

An emotion she didn't recognise flickered in his eyes. 'I think there should be. We have things to say to each other.' Oh...*oh*. Thank goodness.

'What if I fly into Heathrow on Christmas Eve?'

'I'll meet you at the airport,' Millie told him, immediately feeling lighter and brighter. He was coming back, it wasn't the end. All would be well.

'No, that's not necessary. I'll let you know when I'm on my way.' Ben stroked her cheek. 'You've had a hell of a day, darling. Try to relax.'

Yeah, *right*.

'I'm still really nervous, Ben.'

Ben plucked her glass of champagne from her hand and looked at his watch. 'We have ten minutes until we arrive. Let's see if I can change that.'

Millie immediately recognised his expression. She was now easily able to recognise passion when it flared in his eyes. She checked that the privacy screen between them and the driver was in place and held up a hand. 'You can't mess up my hair or make-up, Ben.'

'I'm not going to kiss you, Millie. Well, not on your mouth, anyway.'

He sent her a wicked, wicked grin and ran his hand up and under her skirt, creating streaks of lightning on her skin. His fingers slipped under the brief thong she wore and skimmed over her feminine lips, instantly finding her core. He spread her moisture over her bead and Millie was astounded, as always, at how quickly he could rocket her from zero to gasping.

She dropped her head back against the cool leather seat and widened her legs, not able to believe that Ben was stroking her in the back seat on the way to a very upmarket event.

Ben slipped one finger into her and she gasped at the lovely, lovely intrusion, her channel gripping his fingers. He pulled his hand away and she protested. He impatiently moved her panties to the side and Millie closed her eyes in relief when his middle finger joined his index finger inside her again.

'Look at me,' he commanded her.

Millie opened her eyes and stared into those deep blue-purple depths, mesmerised by the lust she saw in his eyes. She couldn't believe that this amazing man wanted her so much. She could see everything he wanted to do to her in his eyes.

In all that blue, she could see clips of all the times they'd made love, rolling around his bed, in the shower, up against the wall of his hallway when they were too hot for each other to wait until they got inside the house properly.

He took her hand and put it on his steel-hard erection. 'I wish I could lay you down and take you here, right now, but that's further than we can go…right now, at least,' he muttered, his thumb brushing her clitoris in a barely-there stroke. Millie still released a deep moan.

'But I can make you feel good, I can make you feel *amazing*,' Ben told her, placing his lips on the space where her jaw met her neck and gently, gently sucking. 'God, you smell delicious.'

Millie felt herself building and she rocked her hips as Ben increased the stroke of his fingers, the pressure on her bead. She wanted to kiss him, but knew she couldn't, so she concentrated on his fingers, feeling her pleasure building. Her legs felt shaky and her breasts full, and lust shimmered in the air.

'You've got to come now, Mils,' he growled against her skin. 'We're going to be stopping soon.'

Millie heard the warning in his voice and as Ben stroked her harder, she flew apart, encased in a light, bright band of pleasure that spun her away. When she came back to earth, softly panting, Ben was gently wiping her with a cotton handkerchief he'd taken from the inside pocket of his jacket.

She sent him a weak smile and his mouth twitched with amusement. 'Still nervous?' he asked, sounding more than a little smug.

The car was crawling now and Millie lifted her hand to pat her hair. 'Just a little worried about my hair,' she airily told him, inwardly cursing her husky voice.

'You look fine, sweetheart, hair and make-up intact. I am,' Ben loftily and arrogantly informed her, 'damn good at what I do.'

Millie sat in a highchair in a small dressing room somewhere behind the stage, watching her reflection in the mirror as the make-up artist fluttered around her, dusting her nose with powder, and refreshing her lipstick. Bettina had whisked her off, telling her she needed a touch-up before she went on stage. Millie agreed. Her lipstick had faded and one of the curls on the back of her head felt loose.

The make-up artist gave her a shy smile and Millie, needing a couple of minutes to get her thoughts in order, was grateful for her silence. In the few hours, she'd discovered who her father was—a monstrous predator—cried all over Ben, got herself ready for this function, travelled from Ben's house in the limo, had a stunning orgasm, posed for a million photographs, shaken even more hands and smiled.

And smiled. And smiled some more. She'd met a lot of people whose names she had no hope of remembering, she felt emotionally depleted and she longed for a glass of champagne or a stiff whisky.

Millie couldn't wait to get the speech over so she could, metaphorically, let down her hair...

She shouldn't look at the photos projected on to the big screen behind her and on screens all over the theatre, Ben informed her, as they would show heart-tugging photographs of her mum. She wouldn't. They'd been chosen to elicit emotion and the last thing she wanted to do was cry in front of strangers. So, no, she had no intention of looking behind her at the big screen. She'd read her speech and get off the stage.

And then she'd have an enormous glass of champagne.

Millie heard the door behind her open and in the

mirror in front of her saw Bettina slip into the room, carrying a crystal flute, filled with pale gold liquid.

'That had better be for me,' Millie muttered, holding her hand out.

Bettina passed the glass over and Millie took a huge sip. 'Where's Ben?' she asked.

'Pacing the corridor outside. Given his history, he's probably even more nervous than you are now,' Bettina said, resting her hip against the counter running against the wall and below the mirror.

Millie's head jerked and the make-up artist, Anna, groaned when her hand slipped. Millie looked straight ahead again, her eyes connecting with Bettina's in the mirror. 'What do you mean by that?' she asked.

Bettina shifted from foot to foot, looking uncomfortable. 'Um, you know, because of what happened with Margrét?'

What happened? And who was Margrét? 'What are you talking about, Bets?' Millie demanded.

Bettina winced and sent a longing look at the door. It was obvious she was desperate to escape. 'I thought that, given how close you and Ben seem to be, he would've told you...'

Millie glared at her mother's best friend. 'Bets, what do I need to know?'

Bets looked down and ran an elegant finger, red nail polish glistening, around the edge of the glass. 'Didn't he tell you why his engagement ended abruptly?'

Millie's mouth dropped open in surprise. As far

as she knew, he'd only ever had surface-skimming relationships. '*Ben* was engaged?'

'Did you not know?'

No, she bloody well didn't! How could she not know? And why, when Ben knew all her deepest secrets, hadn't he told her? 'When was this?'

Bettina waved her hand in the air. 'Oh, a few years before your mum died. He was pretty young, but so in love. She came from a very wealthy, very connected family.'

Anna stepped back, declared she was done, but Millie couldn't be bothered with her appearance.

Mille wanted to scream with frustration when someone called Bettina's name and she hurried away, looking relieved to be let off the conversational hook.

Damn, because she wanted to know more about Ben and his broken engagement. Over the past two weeks, she'd told him so much about her childhood—and her future hopes and dreams—but Ben had shared very little about his past. Millie could think of at least ten occasions when he could've mentioned he'd been engaged and that he'd once thought about marriage. She'd even asked him whether he'd ever been in love, but he never answered her.

He never answered her...

She was a gushing geyser; he was a hidden away ice cave. He was aware of how much her mum's secrets had hurt her and knew how insecure she felt as a child, knowing she wasn't loved by Magnús and not knowing why. She'd cried all over him, told him about her father, exposed herself and shown him her soft underbelly but he didn't feel enough for her, or didn't trust her enough, to show her his. He loved her body and enjoyed her mind, but he kept his heart safely tucked away.

He hadn't been dishonest, but neither had he been truly honest, and that realisation was hard to swallow. They said that girls fell in love with men who were either like, or the exact opposite, of their fathers. Ben, in his inability to communicate, was very like the man she grew up with. Like Magnús, he kept himself emotionally isolated.

She was having an affair with her husband and was in love with him, but he couldn't emotionally engage with her. She needed more than surface, she always had. She'd never been able to break through Magnús's reserves to find the man behind the armour and it seemed as though she was repeating that mistake with Ben.

It was possible she was banging on a door that would never open.

Her choices were to keep banging, hoping it opened a crack and she could slip in through, or to give up on trying to get him to confide in her. Which way to jump? Right? Left? Not at all?

They'd agreed to talk later…could she talk about this?

She knew what she wanted and that was to carry on seeing him. Would he want to continue their relationship if she asked? But was what they had, right now, *enough*? He was her best friend, her confidant, but she didn't want to keep taking, she wanted to give as well. She wanted him to confide in her, to be his best friend, to support him when he needed propping up.

But would he open up if she asked him to? Could he? If he couldn't, and if she wanted Ben in her life, then she'd have to accept his emotional distance. Could she live with him being like that? Could she have someone in her life who knew everything about her, but she knew nothing of him? She didn't know...

Millie knew she didn't want to spend the rest of her life begging him to let her in. She knew how it felt to be continuously rebuffed, how frustrating and soul-destroying it could be. If Ben couldn't give her what she needed, then it might be better for her, better for *them*, if they called it over...

It would hurt—she loved him, how could she not?—but she could walk away. She *would*. She had to because she'd fought this battle before and it had dented and damaged her.

But before she did anything too drastic, said words she couldn't take back, she and Ben needed to talk. She wanted a relationship with him, but he'd have to emotionally unbend.

She couldn't be the only one with emotional skin in the game.

CHAPTER TEN

BEN STOOD IN the wings on the impressive stage, shoved his hands into his suit pockets and watched as Millie walked to the podium on what he knew were shaky legs. Millie had asked him to come backstage with her and he'd agreed, knowing she needed his support.

Public speaking, especially at such an important event, was always hard, but talking about your dead mum was doubly so. If he could do it for her, he would, but he couldn't take the chance.

He didn't know if, as soon as he spoke Jacqui's name, emotion would flood his system and his words would disappear. He didn't know if he'd stammer the first few sentences and then dry up. He couldn't risk freezing, embarrassing himself and spoiling the evening for everyone else. He wouldn't do that to Millie, or to Jacqui's memory. No, he was in the right place.

Ben noticed the hesitation in her usually fluid steps. Nerves had taken hold of her again and he couldn't blame her, he felt as though his were also on fire. Honestly, he felt as though he was perching

on the rim of the volcanic crater this stunning auditorium, Eldborg, was named after. The auditorium,
built in concrete and covered with red-varnished
birch veneer, reflected his red-hot inner core.

He had to calm down. If he didn't, he would trans-
fer his nerves to Millie, and she was jumpy enough
as it was. Ben took a deep breath and looked across
the orchestra to where rows of elegantly and expen-
sively dressed patrons sat. The woman wore Dior
and Givenchy, Armani and Chanel and the men wore
custom-made tuxedos from Brioni, Tom Ford and
Cesare Attollini.

Behind the podium, and on strategic places
throughout the hall, were screens so that the guests
in the cheap seats didn't have to watch a tiny Millie
speak. The screen would show images of Jacqui as
Millie gave her moving tribute to her mum. There
were words on the teleprompter and all she had to do
was get through the next fifteen minutes.

Ben looked at his wife, his lover, thinking how
stunning she looked. She looked like the heiress she
was, elegant and sophisticated and lovely. But she
was also kind and accepting and non-judgemental.

He'd thought he'd been so smart thinking he could
control his emotions when it came to her. Another
woman maybe, but not Millie. Had he grabbed on
to the idea of linking his emotions to his stuttering
as a way to rationalise keeping her around? Had his
subconscious looked for a way to keep her by his
side? Did it know, instinctively, that she was the one
person, the only woman, he could imagine having

a deep relationship with, even a measure of permanence, and he was searching for a way to keep her in his life?

Yeah…

His stammer now seemed relatively unimportant, keeping his feelings under control less so. He could even imagine giving her the baby she so desperately wanted. He might even be able to be a dad. He knew he wanted to try…

With Millie to guide him, he could do this. And if his kid stuttered—no he couldn't go there, not yet. Not now…

But in the future, yes. Ben was starting to believe that, with Millie at his side, he could do anything. There was no way they were done…not yet. Not for the next sixty or so years.

He watched as Millie cleared her throat and touched the slender microphone. He mentally urged her to start talking—the longer she stood there, the more her nerves would take hold. He silently urged her to start the speech, his fists bunched at his sides.

Just don't look at the screens, Mils, and don't watch the photos.

But Millie, being Millie, did exactly that. He silently cursed when the first picture hit the screens. It was a favourite of his. It was a candid shot of Jacq and Millie, who was probably around ten, sitting on the beach, laughing uproariously. It was clear that they not only loved each other, but took enormous pleasure in each other's company. It was a highly emotive and beautiful shot.

The picture on the screen flipped over to one of Jacq holding Millie, shortly after she was born, a red-faced baby with lots of hair. Jacqui, sweaty and make-up free, was laughing, triumph and love blazing from her eyes. It was another intensely emotional picture and one he knew would hit Millie hard. This picture had been taken just a few months after she was beaten up by her ex. If Millie started thinking about the past, her biological father, she'd collapse in a heap.

He watched, horrified, as she looked at the picture and despair jumped into her eyes. She lifted her fist to her mouth and Ben heard the collective intake of the audience. Everyone was on the edge of their seats, waiting to see what happened next. Millie dragged her eyes off the screen and her head whipped around, and Ben knew she was looking for him. Their eyes connected and held, and Ben saw the unspoken words on her face…

I can't do this. Please help me.

If he had to, he would do that damn speech for her, he would stutter and stammer his way through it, but Jacqui would be honoured. Without giving himself time to think, Ben strode on to the stage, keeping his eyes locked on Millie's face. He reached her, placed his hand on her back and bent to speak in her ear. 'Can you do this? Or must I?'

Please let her say she could.

He held his breath as he waited for her answer. Then he felt her spine straighten. She tipped her head back to speak in his ear, so softly that the microphone couldn't pick up her words. 'I want to try, for her. Can you stand next to me and, if I fumble, can you pick it up from me?'

'Always,' Ben assured her and she had no way of knowing he'd do it in every way he could, for as long as she would let him.

Millie heard the thundering applause in her ears as she walked off the stage, Ben's hand on her back. Her head buzzed with a million thoughts. She'd got through her speech without crying, she'd done her mum proud and the audience liked what she had to say. The hardest part of her evening was over. Well, until Ben left.

Dammit.

'I'm so damn proud of you, Mils,' he told her, ducking his head to kiss her mouth.

When he stood again, he had lipstick on his top lip and Millie lifted her thumb to wipe it away. The tears she'd been holding back threatened to spill and she blinked rapidly. 'Thank you.'

'I wish I didn't have to leave tonight. All I want to do is take you home, strip all that gold material off you and spend the rest of the night making love to you,' Ben softly stated, looking frustrated.

She held her breath and saw her feelings in his eyes. Maybe she wouldn't have to say anything, maybe... 'Ben, we really need to talk.'

He cupped the side of her face with his big hand and rested his forehead against hers. 'I know, sweetheart. There's much to say and we'd be having that conversation tonight if I didn't have to rush off. I'd stay if I could.'

'You made a commitment and you've already missed tonight's celebrations,' Millie told him. 'I'm grateful to you for being here. I couldn't have done that without you.'

'Of course you could, you are amazing.' Millie heard someone calling her name and she sighed as Ben dropped his hand and stepped away from her. He looked past her shoulder and grimaced.

'There are hordes of people, including Bettina and some of the trustees, waiting to congratulate you.'

She'd rather lie down in a bed of fire ants. And they only had a half-hour before the concert was about to start. 'I don't want to spend the little time I have left with you watching a concert. Will our absence be noticed?' she asked as he steered her away from Bettina's group. Ben was leaving directly after the concert and she…

Did not.

Want him.

To go.

'Since we are seated in the front row, in the middle, with trustees on either side of us, I'd say yes,' Ben told her, his smile warm but frustrated.

'Damn.' She slipped her hand into his and rested her head against his shoulder as he steered her down a few steps into a quieter area empty of guests. 'I could do with a drink.'

He walked over to a waiter in the distance and returned with two glasses of champagne, then led Millie through a series of doors before finding a small, empty room and pulling her inside.

Ben lowered his head to kiss her and Millie sighed when his lips hit hers. She waited to be swept away, to fall into the magic of their kiss, but an annoying imp shouted questions from her shoulder.

Did he kiss her—Margrét—like this? How much did he love her? Did he still think about her?

She pulled back and Ben squinted down at her. 'What's the matter?' he asked.

She needed the answer to one question now—curiosity was burning a hole through her stomach. 'Why didn't you tell me you were engaged?' Millie asked him.

He quietly cursed and she knew he didn't want to answer her question. Doubts, hot and sour, rolled over her. It was all very well saying that they should talk, to find a way forward, but was she setting herself up for disappointment? If Ben couldn't talk to her about his ex, someone she presumed he was over, then what hope was there for him opening up about everything else?

Fear invaded her body. What was she doing? She was risking her heart, risking getting hurt…

Ben frowned. 'I didn't think it was relevant and it was a long time ago.' He touched the frown lines between her eyebrows. 'Why are we talking about this now?'

Because she needed some reassurance to get her through the next few days apart? 'I hate that you don't talk to me, Ben. And I don't feel as though you were honest with me.'

'I never lied to you,' he countered.

'I asked you if you'd ever been in love,' she shot back. 'It was a perfect time to tell me you'd been engaged, to explain what happened. You loving someone else isn't a big deal, you not telling me you were engaged *is*.'

'I'm not good at expressing myself, Mils,' he replied, sounding frustrated. She didn't blame him—he'd come in here to spend some time loving her, wanting to give her a send-off that'd carry them through the next few days, but she was throwing up barriers between them.

'I know, but I wish you would try,' Millie said, sounding a little desperate. 'I've lived with half-truths and I hate feeling as though I'm standing on shifting sand. I need to know everything, the good, bad and ugly.'

Oh, stop, Millie. Just let it go.

But she couldn't. The floodgates were open and she couldn't hold back the tide.

Ben lifted his arm and rested it against the wall above her head. Millie looked up into his masculine face.

Her breath caught at the emotion in his eyes—there was something there she'd never seen before. Something softer, kinder, but also bolder and braver. 'Are you sure you want the truth, Mils?'

'Always,' she assured him, her heart speeding up

at the tenderness in his eyes. Was he about to…? Could she hope that he…?

Ben rested his forehead against hers. It took him a few minutes to speak. 'There are so many things I want to s-say, Millie, b-but we have so…so little time,' he said, his voice deeper than usual. 'I…I… th-think… Ca-ca-ca-*crap*!'

He hauled in a deep breath, closed his eyes and Millie's eyebrows raised. He looked as though he was in physical pain. What was going on with him?

'La-la-*look*,' Ben spat the last word out with the speed of a bullet. His F-bomb came out far more fluently than any of his words before.

'Are you okay?'

'Of ca-ca-course I…I'm bl-bl-bloody okay!'

She'd never seen him like this, abruptly distressed and flustered and upset. She was so used to Ben being controlled and urbane and she didn't recognise the wild look in his eyes and didn't know the reason for the heat in his cheeks. 'Seriously, Ben, what's wrong?' she asked, gripping his arm. 'Should I call someone?'

He whipped his head back and forth in what she presumed was a sharp no. 'Okay, I won't call anyone. Yet. But only if you relax and take a couple of deep breaths.'

Another very fluent, very loud curse bounced off the wall and Millie took a step back, not understanding his anger. She lifted her hands and stepped back further, feeling as though she was walking through a field planted with landmines.

Ben jammed his hands into the pockets of his pants, misery and horror on his face. Then he dropped his hands and shoved his hands into his hair, whirling away from her. Frowning, she stared at his big back and lifted and bit down hard on her bottom lip. What was going on here?

She stepped towards him and placed her hand on his back, utterly confused. 'Ben?'

He shrugged her hand off and walked away from her. She watched as he put both hands on a wall and dropped his head. Every muscle in his body tensed— he was a pulled-too-tight cable about to snap. She wanted to go to him, to wrap her arms around his waist and tell him that everything would be okay, but knew he needed her to keep her distance.

She just wished she understood. Just a few minutes ago he was kissing her, now he was emotional and upset. All she could give him was time…

But they didn't have much of it.

After what felt like an age, but was only a few minutes, Ben straightened. He turned around, did up the button to his dinner jacket and when he finally lifted his head, she saw that Cool and Collected Ben was back. He looked as though the past few minutes hadn't happened and when their eyes met, all his many barriers were back in place.

He lifted his arm and made a production of looking at his watch. 'I think we should go, the concert will be starting shortly.'

Millie stared at him, flabbergasted. Would he walk away from her without an explanation? Oh, no, they were not going to brush his odd behaviour under the mat.

'Shall we?' Ben asked in his smooth, nothing-to-see-here voice and gestured to the door.

'No.'

When his eyebrows raised, giving her a look that suggested she was being unreasonable, she lifted her chin. 'Ben, darling, I don't understand. I'm worried about you—your reaction is completely out of character. I need to know what just happened.'

His eyes dropped from hers, for just a second. 'Nothing happened, Millie.'

'And you say that you are honest with me! Are you kidding me?' She released her own milder curse and slapped her arms against her chest. 'No, you don't just get to act the way you did and then walk away without an explanation, Jónsson!'

'What the hell do you want from me, Millie?' Ben shouted, that cool mask falling away.

'I want you to tell me what just happened, I want you to open up! I want you to talk to me!' Millie shouted back.

Ben looked furious, but still so, so cool. Cold anger was so much scarier than an overheated temper. 'Okay, so do you want me to tell you that I stutter, that I've always stuttered? There have been times when I haven't been able to form a sentence or make any sense. I've heard more "just relax" and "take a breath" comments than you've had cups of coffee!'

Sure, she'd caught the odd stammer, nothing serious, and he didn't stutter as a rule. 'I have never heard you stutter until a few minutes ago,' she told him. 'I never suspected it.'

'That's because I've worked damn hard to overcome it because it's not part of who I am any more,' Ben whipped back. 'Here's the honesty you want… I stutter when I'm emotional, when I feel too much. It's always worse when I'm upset or when I'm feeling overwhelmed or out of control.'

She was trying to make sense of what he was saying, trying to sort his words into concepts she could understand. She shrugged her shoulders and lifted her hands. 'Stuttering is *not* a big deal, Ben.'

Her words were barely out when she'd realised, once again, she'd said the wrong thing. His eyes turned a violent shade of purple and two strips of pink coloured his cheekbones. He took a couple of deep breaths—closed his eyes—and pulled out his phone. He scrolled through it and eventually held up the phone so she could see the screen.

Ben was a child in the video, maybe eleven or twelve, tall and gangly and as pale as a ghost. She saw the tracks left by tears on his cheeks, but his eyes were full of defiance as he tried to read from the book he held in his hand. Every word was torture and she only understood every couple of words. His sentences made no sense at all.

'It's all a matter of mind over matter, Benedikt! If you decide not to stutter, you won't,' a strident voice coming from his phone's speakers made her jump. His mother, she presumed. 'My teachers assure me that you're not stupid, but, right now, I have my doubts.'

Millie closed her eyes, feeling lava-hot anger run through her. How could his mum speak to him in that way? How could she be so cruel and heartless?

Ben jabbed a finger at his screen. 'That's who I was, that's how I spoke when I was a child. Sometimes it was much worse. That's how I get when I allow emotions to get in the way! I will *not*—I refuse to go back to being that person again!'

Millie felt as though she was still walking through that field of landmines, uncertain of what path to take. 'You worked so hard to overcome it, Ben.'

'You'd think, right? I thought so, too, until I stood at my engagement party, trying to make a toast to my bride, who I was crazy about, and my first sentence was a train wreck. She dumped me a few days later, telling me she didn't think we were suited. I knew it was because I embarrassed her that night.'

'Why do you think I refused to do that speech for you?' Ben demanded, his tone still as harsh as the wind flying off the Langjökull glacier. 'It's because I loved your mum and I knew I'd become emotional. And when I become emotional, I stutter. When I stutter, I feel...'

His words trailed away, and Millie didn't need him to fill in the blanks, to connect the dots. When he stuttered he felt out of control, as though he was a kid again, as though he was in that space where he thought nothing would ever be okay again.

'Your stutter does not make you *unlovable*,' she insisted.

Ben didn't take in her words. 'After Margrét, it was easy to work out that emotion and my stutter are inexplicably intertwined and I vowed I would never allow my relationships to go more than surface deep,' he stated.

But he'd stuttered with her earlier. What did that mean? 'But you have feelings for me,' Millie said, taking a stab in the dark.

He nodded, not bothering to deny her claim. Instead, he simply shrugged. 'And that's why I'm walking out of here, jumping on my plane and going to St Barth's. And why I won't be spending Christmas with you or having any contact with you in the future. Nor will I give you a child. It's not going to happen, Millie. I can't do this, I can't do *any* of it.'

Just like that? Did he really think she was going to stand for such a bloody awful explanation? 'Oh, that's such a cop-out, Jónsson, you are such a coward!'

Anger suffused his features and the blood drained from his face. 'What did you say to me? How dare you?' he asked her through clenched teeth. 'Do you know how long it took me to get my stuttering under control? Do you know how many tears I shed, how many walls I punched, and how often I screamed and shouted in my head when my words got stuck in my throat?

'I had no support from my parents—my mum

thought I wasn't trying hard enough—my dad simply believed it would come right on its own and I had to find my own counsellors and my therapists! I'm *not* a coward!'

'You are if you are keeping it from letting you love me,' Millie told him. It wasn't a good time to tell him that, despite never having seen him so angry or out of control, she'd yet to hear him stutter. Yeah, he might have a couple of words go amiss here and there, but if he could yell at her without stuttering, then he could love her without it being a problem, too.

'And I think you might love me, Ben. I love you,' she stated. 'And I'm so furious that you've put this barrier between us when there was no need to do that. I'm so angry that you couldn't tell me that you stuttered and that you kept this from me.'

'I won't discuss my speech impediment, Millie.'

Ben looked away, but his stubborn expression remained. She knew how obstinate and determined he could be—he hadn't built an international empire without deciding on a course of action and pursuing it with zeal. He looked at his watch again. 'You should get back to the concert,' he told her.

It was obvious he was emotionally retreating and even more obvious he wasn't going to join her in the front row to watch the gala concert. *Marvellous.* Nor would he come to see her in London. Millie felt her throat tighten and remembered long-ago conversations with Magnús, wondering why she could never break through, wondering why he couldn't love her, wondering what was wrong with her. And here she was again, standing in front of a man, begging him to love her, and, once again, she was being batted away.

She was done. She couldn't give her love to someone who didn't want it. But before she walked away, she had more to say.

'I want to say a few things and I'll hope you'll give me the courtesy of hearing me out,' she said, hearing the wobble in her voice and hating herself. 'I cannot tell you how little I care that you stutter. I'm sorry you went through such a torrid time as a child, but you've been shouting at me, emotion blazing, without stuttering once, so I'm wondering if it's as bad as you think it is.

'So you got choked up and your words didn't come quickly enough. So *what*? Again, your stutter does not make you less you, less lovable, less anything. If you couldn't speak at all, I would still love you. I think I always have,' she said, sounding sad. 'You've never let me down...until today.'

She blinked and couldn't help the single tear that slid down her face. 'I trusted you to tell me the truth, but you held back and you didn't trust me with this. And that hurts, so much. Secondly, you are the best person in my life and over these past two weeks, I've come to love you. But I will not beg you to trust me or to love me. I did that with Magnús and I nearly destroyed myself in the process.

'It's your choice to love me or not, Benedikt, your choice to stay on your emotional island or to join the rest of us who are prepared to flounder our way through love. Be alone or be with me but...' she swallowed and looked him dead in the eye '…if you are with me, then you are *with* me. And that includes talking to me, letting me in. I'm not prepared to keep banging on the door, demanding entrance into your inner world.'

He rubbed his hand over his mouth, up his jaw, and Millie saw the misery in his eyes. 'I can't, Millie. You're asking too much.'

No, she wasn't. But she couldn't make him see that.

She wasn't going to cry, not yet. She still had to walk out of this room with her dignity intact and sit through a concert. She could cry later, on the plane back to London tomorrow. She couldn't cry here.

'Okay, then,' she told him and heard her voice crack. She needed to leave now, before she begged him not to throw her away. Faced with the immensity of her need for him, with the reality of what she was walking away from, she wanted to grovel to him to keep her. She fought the urge to tell him she'd accept anything he could give her.

But, if she did, in time she'd come to resent him, just as she had Magnús. No, it was better to walk away. Millie forced herself to kiss his cheek, to touch his cheek with her fingertips. 'Take care, Benedikt.'

Gathering every bit of courage she possessed, she walked out of the empty room they'd taken refuge in.

CHAPTER ELEVEN

EDEN ROCK HAD been voted one of the best hotels in the world and every time he came here, Ben was reminded why. The setting, being right on the beach, was perfect, the service was exceptional and the amenities were varied and wonderful. With golf, tennis and a range of water sports on offer, it was also a perfect spot to host a stag weekend for a group of guys who liked to be active, but who weren't into pub crawling and getting wasted.

He'd arrived in St Barth's mid-morning two days ago, just in time to be included in a round of golf and from there he and his friends hit the beach, finding that Anders had arranged jet skis for them. They'd spent the next two hours on the water, had a quick shower and met up again for drinks on the terrace and then an exceptional supper. Then, to toast the groom-to-be, they got stuck into the hotel's exceptional wine and whisky list.

He hadn't thought about Millie or the train wreck he left behind in Reykjavik. Or, more accurately, he tried not to. And every time he felt his heart splitting in two, he had another glass of wine or threw back another whisky.

As a result, he felt like death warmed up. So sick and so sad. Ben walked out of the warm, clear sea and pushed back his hair, wishing Millie was by his side, or that she was waiting for him in their room, or on a lounger or at the breakfast table. He wished he could make his life with her, take a chance on her, wished he could believe that their love would last for ever, through thick and thin, through stammers and stutters.

She'd told him she didn't give a damn about his speech impediment, that it meant no more to her than the birthmark on his thigh, or the scar on his chin, did. But how could he believe that when it meant so much to him? How could she brush away something that defined the way he lived his life? It was the barrier he'd erected between him and the world, the impenetrable bulletproof glass shield excuse that didn't allow him to emotionally engage.

Ben picked a towel off the lounger and roughly swiped his chest, before sitting on the lounger, inspecting the fine-grained sand between his feet. He didn't want to be here, the sun hot on his shoulders and the gentle wind ruffling his hair. He wanted to be in London, wet and drizzly, or in snowy Iceland. He wanted to be with Millie.

But being with Millie meant being vulnerable, opening himself up and taking a chance she wouldn't hurt him.

Olivier and Anders, walked towards him, dressed,

like he was, only in board shorts. They both wore dark sunglasses and Ben wished he'd thought to pick up his own before leaving his luxury room. His eyes felt as though they were being slowly roasted on an open fire.

'Ben, we are flying out just after lunch. What time are you leaving?' Anders asked when they stopped to speak to him. Ben looked up at him and shrugged. It was Christmas Eve tonight and he was supposed to fly to the UK, but he hadn't thought of an alternative arrangement.

'I'm not sure,' he told Anders. 'I might hang around for another day or two and solo celebrate your last few days of being an unmarried man.'

Anders, always so serious, tapped his temple with his index finger. 'I've been a married man, in my heart, since I met Jules. These few days with my friends are just a nice break and not a goodbye to my old way of thinking.'

Ben looked up at him, as his words settled on his skin. He understood what Anders was trying to say—he'd married Jules, emotionally, five years ago and all they were doing with their wedding was making it legal and celebrating their love. He and Mille had made things legal a long time ago, but they'd only discovered each other on an emotional level recently. She'd said she was in love with him, he knew he loved her.

He just didn't know if love was *enough*.

Anders told them he had to find some aspirin for his pounding head and left him and Olivier alone.

His cousin dropped to sit on the sand in front of him and extended his long legs. He leaned back on his hands, beach sand covering his fingers.

'On a scale of one to ten, how rough are you feeling?' Olivier asked him.

'Fifteen,' Ben replied.

'Is that from the booze or because you walked out of the gala concert and left Millie to watch it alone?' Olivier asked, keeping his tone low.

Ben jerked his head and immediately wished he hadn't. He groaned. 'How do you know that?'

'I've seen the articles. You stormed out of the concert hall into your waiting limo, Millie returned to her seat. And every paper, printed and on-line, published a photograph of a devastated-looking Millie sitting next to your empty seat.'

Ben cursed and rubbed his face with both his hands. When he'd left the Harpa Concert Hall, desperate to get away from her and his feelings, he hadn't considered that the gala concert was one of the most covered events of the year, that social diarists and journalists from all over Europe attended the event.

Millie's speech was a big deal. His coming on to the stage to support her, and the intimacy of the gesture, would've raised their *Is love in the air?* suspicions. His bolting, just a half-hour later, would've added fuel to their journalistic fire. *Dammit.* This situation had gone from bad to worse to terrible.

'Millie had to fight her way through a group of journalists outside your house when she left for the airport,' Olivier told him. 'There were more photo-graphs of her in the papers.'

'How did she look?'

'Hard to tell because she was wearing enormous sunglasses and a floppy hat.' Olivier shrugged. 'But pale. She looked pale.'

Ben cursed again, keeping his tone low because kids were running past him and he didn't want them to learn words they shouldn't.

'So, what happened, Benedikt?'

Ben told him about their fight, that he'd started to stutter, his terror when emotion swamped him. He couldn't allow emotion back into his life because if he did, he would start to stutter again and he refused to allow that to happen.

Olivier tipped his head to the side, looking con-fused. 'So, you started to stutter at the beginning of your argument with Millie?'

'Mmm,' Ben replied, feeling twelve again. He dragged his foot through the sand.

'So you stuttered, told her you couldn't be with her and left, right?'

'No, we argued. She told me she loved me, that we could be together, that she didn't care about my stutter,' Ben explained. 'Can we stop talking about this now?'

'No,' Olivier retorted. 'And you argued for how long?'

Been shrugged. 'Ten minutes, fifteen? Twenty? I can't remember, we both had a lot to say.'

'And did you stutter while you were arguing with her?' Olivier asked.

The question punched Ben between his eyeballs. He stared at his cousin as the importance of his words sank in. 'No. I was fine.'

Olivier rolled his eyes at him. 'So you had a quick relapse, but kept fighting with her because a couple of sentences came out wrong? You broke her heart over a *couple* of sentences?'

Words, not sentences. But he wasn't going to help Olivier make his case. Ben sighed and gripped the bridge of his nose with his finger and thumb. When Olivier put it like that, it sounded stupid. *He* sounded stupid. He thought he should try to explain why he was running from Millie. Maybe if it made sense to Olivier, it would make sense to him. 'Emotion scares me. I was feeling emotional and I started to stutter. If I don't nip this in the bud now, I might regress.'

Olivier's look suggested he'd been out in the sun for too long. 'Get real, Ben, we both know that's not going to happen. You've worked far too hard and too long to let that happen. And if you stutter with the people who care about you, who the hell cares? The people who love you—me, Millie—love you whether you stutter or not. Heads up, perfect speech is not a requirement to be loved.'

Millie said the same thing, love wasn't conditional. But could he believe it? His mum was supposed to love him, but she couldn't. Neither could Margrét. Ben bit his lip and shook his head. 'Lo-lo-love hurts, Olivier. It's hurt m-me.'

'No, *love* didn't hurt you. Your mother, because she had the emotional range of a crowbar, hurt you. Margrét, because she was more concerned about how your relationship looked to the outside world, hurt you. But do you know what hurts more, Ben?' Olivier demanded, sitting up and resting his arms on his now bent knees. 'Loneliness hurts. Rejection hurts. Walking away because you're an idiot hurts. Trying to protect yourself hurts. We blame love for hurting us, but it doesn't. Love doesn't hurt. Love heals those wounds and fixes the bumps. It gets you through the day.'

Ben met his cousin, and best friend's, eyes. He couldn't speak, partly because emotion was bubbling in his throat and if he tried to push words past that mess, he'd make a mess of what he was trying to say.

'You've been married to that girl for twelve years, Ben, and I've never seen you happier than I have these past few weeks. You might not have known it at the time, but she was always the girl you were supposed to be with.'

He shook his head. 'I d-don't know, Ol.'

'Of course you do,' Olivier told him, ignoring his stammer. 'You're just being stubborn. You want to love her, you want to be with her, you want to spend your life with her, but you're scared of taking that leap, of being emotionally vulnerable.' Olivier reached across the sand and punched his thigh. Hard. *Dammit, ow!*

'Pull your head out of your—' He saw a little girl building a sandcastle quite close to them and adjusted his words. 'Out of the sand and go and be with her. Throw your lot in with hers and see what happens.'

'What h-happens if it f-falls apart?' Ben asked, terrified at the idea.

Olivier shrugged. 'Then your heart gets shattered and you can go back to being the introverted, unemotional robot you were before.'

'I feel like that now,' Ben reluctantly admitted, rubbing his aching thigh.

'Then you might as well take a punt and be happy before you feel like that again,' Olivier cheerfully told him. 'But I don't think that's going to happen. I suspect that when Millie jumps in, she does it with both feet and all of her body.'

Ben took the hand Olivier held out and allowed his cousin to pull him to his feet. 'I'll think about what you said,' he told Olivier.

Olivier shook his blond head. 'No, you and thinking are a dangerous combination. Just tell your pilot to get your jet ready, get to the airport and fly to London. When you get there, go to Millie. She'll do the rest...'

'Your faith in me is touching,' Ben told him, his tone dry as they walked back to the hotel.

Olivier grinned at him. 'And tell Millie to let me know whether I should withdraw your divorce petition. And for God's sake, buy the woman a ring, Jónsson. Actually, *don't*, she's a jewellery designer, you'll probably get it wrong. Let her choose her own.'

Ben stopped and rolled his eyes. When Olivier finally stopped talking, he shook his head. 'Are you done telling me what to do?' he asked, a little bemused by this volley of instructions.

Olivier slapped his hand on his back and the movement propelled Ben forward. 'I intend to be your shadow until I get you on your plane and see you taking off. I'm not letting you bail, Cousin.'

Ben didn't think he would. Living with his fear might be hard, but living without Millie was impossible. 'Why don't you organise your own love life and stay out of mine?' Ben grumbled.

'Where's the fun in that?' Olivier demanded, laughing.

Millie aimlessly wandered around her top-floor Notting Hill apartment, feeling unsettled and off balance. Nothing, it turned out, stopped the ache of a broken heart. Her entire body was slowly crumbling and she was a hostage to sadness. Since she watched Ben walk out of her life, her nerves started vibrating at a higher intensity and every bump, scrape or bruise was so much more painful than anything she'd experienced before. Her heart was shattered and so was her spirit.

She'd been hurt when Magnús rejected her and by her mum's inability to tell her who her father was. Discovering the identity of her real father upset her, but Ben choosing not to love her was pain on an industrial scale.

What made their situation worse was that she knew he felt something for her—it might not be love, but it was close—and she couldn't believe he'd chosen to walk away from her, dismissing all they could be. He was choosing loneliness and solitude over her and that added a layer to hurt she'd never experienced before.

How could he think that being miserable and lonely was better than being together?

Millie looked out of her window on to the street below, taking in the flickering light of a Christmas tree in the window of the flat opposite. It was Christmas Eve and she was spending it alone. For once she didn't mind—if she couldn't be with Ben, then she preferred to be by herself.

She could cry in peace, she wouldn't have to put on a happy and pretend to be jolly.

Millie placed the balls of her hands into her eye sockets and pushed back her tears. She'd cried more over the last two days than she had since her mum died and knew her red nose could rival Rudolph's. Her hair was a tangled mess and she wore her most comfortable pair of yoga pants, thick fluffy socks and a sweatshirt of Ben's she'd nicked from his closet.

She should eat, but whatever she swallowed immediately wanted out. She wasn't sure if a broken heart or starvation would kill her first.

Stupid, *stupid* man for not giving them a chance.

Later, she'd try to eat tea and toast. Tomorrow she'd eat something more substantial. The day after tomorrow her heart would feel a tiny bit better and it would start to heal in minuscule increments. Because, even though it didn't feel like that right now,

Millie was mature enough to know her heart would, in some way, heal. She would smile again. Not today or tomorrow, possibly not next week or next year, but at some point, she'd learn to live again. She hoped.

And in the New Year, she would force herself to choose a sperm donor from the website, she would go to the clinic and be artificially inseminated. Hopefully, she'd fall pregnant straight away, but if she didn't she would try again. She would continue with her pre-Ben plans—they were good plans and made sense. Married or divorced or separated, Ben or no Ben, she wasn't putting her dreams on hold any longer. Not for any man.

She needed a family, someone to love. She wanted a child, she wanted children. It was a pity that Ben couldn't get past his fear to share her life, and her his, and share children with her. But she wouldn't let him derail her plans.

She would be okay. Not today, but at some point.

Millie rested her head against the window, noticing the low dark clouds. They were predicting snow in London, just a few flakes, but after experiencing an Icelandic blizzard, she wasn't even marginally concerned or impressed. A black London taxi turned down her street, moving slowly along the road, before pulling up next to her flat. Some lucky person in her building, or maybe in the one next door, was home for Christmas…

Millie watched as the door opened and she placed a trembling hand on the cold pane when she saw a big foot, covered in a trendy trainer, hit the pavement. Ben had a pair of trainers just like those. She closed her eyes and rested her forehead on the glass. She had to stop thinking about him…she was driving herself mad.

When she opened her eyes again, she saw flat, fluffy snowflakes cascading past her window and a tall man stood next to the taxi, a small overnight bag in his hand. Her eyes travelled up his body—jeans, a navy pullover, a black scarf and a camel-coloured coat and, taking in his messy hair and tired, oh-so-familiar face, her heart started to gallop.

Ben stood below her window and he was looking up at her, his face pale in the fading afternoon light. She stared down at him, wondering if she was hallucinating, possibly caused by her lack of food, sleep and extreme sadness.

But then he lifted his hand and pointed to her door, silently asking if he could come up. Millie nodded and a few seconds later her intercom buzzed. Was this really happening? Ben's deep voice sounded a little strained. 'Can I come up? We need to talk.'

'The last time you said that ended in you walking out of my life,' Millie told him, cursing her shaky voice.

'Mils, I'm cold and tired. Let me in, dammit.'

Millie hit the button to unlock the downstairs door and went to her front door and opened it. She heard the sound of Ben's feet as he jogged up the wooden stairs and she swallowed, wondering why he was here and what he would say.

Leaning against the door frame of her front door,

she waited until he reached her landing, her heart pounding at a million beats per second.

Ben stopped in front of her and used his free hand to rake back his hair, dislodging a melting snowflake. He looked as though he hadn't slept any more than she had.

She gestured for him to follow her into her flat and reminded herself she wasn't looking her best either.

Ben closed the door behind him and she turned to look at him. He dropped his overnight bag to the floor and jammed his hands into his coat pockets.

'Coffee? Tea? A drink?' she asked.

He took a long time to answer her and when he finally spoke, he only uttered one word. 'You.'

Ben kept his eyes on Millie's face, taking in the various emotions skittering across her face. With Millie, even if it was on a second-to-second basis, you could always tell how she was feeling if you looked quickly enough. Hope flared first, then delight, then worry and resignation.

Shaking her head, she walked out of her bright and happy sitting room—cream couches with bright cushions, lots of plants and colourful Persian carpets on the old wooden floors—and he followed her slim figure to her small, equally light kitchen. He stood in the doorway while she fiddled with her kettle and reached for two mugs. It looked as though he was getting coffee whether he wanted it or not.

He took in the tension in her slim back and noticed her shoulders were up around her ears. He'd hurt her, and, for that, he was truly sorry. He would make damn sure he never did it again.

If she gave him the chance.

'I'll give you a baby, Millie.'

He knew, as soon as the words left his mouth, he'd said the wrong thing. She whirled around, waving the mug around. 'Thanks, but no thanks.'

He moved over to where she stood and gently removed the mug from her hand. This small apartment was too small for what he wanted to say—he needed more space for the big, important words he intended to say—so he took her hand and pulled her out of the kitchen and back into her much bigger lounge. Knowing he couldn't make her sit, he stood in front of her and looked down into her lovely, much-loved face.

'I'd like to give you a baby, Millie. But I'd like to love you more, share your life, be your lover and husband, be the father of your kids.'

She looked up at him and he saw the disbelief in her eyes.

'You told me that you couldn't, that you'd never allow yourself to become emotionally involved,' Millie said, pulling her hands out of his and walking over to the window. She sat on the narrow window ledge. When he looked up earlier and saw her standing in the window, his heart settled down from a galloping rush into a steady beat. She was what he needed. Having her in his life, whether that life was in Iceland or England, or anywhere else, was all that mattered.

He could only say the words and hope she believed them. He'd keep saying them, badly and over and over again, until he got them right. 'I love you, Millicent.'

Millie heard the three simple words, felt them settle on her skin and hauled in a deep breath. She fought the urge to fly to him, to wind her arms around his waist and bury her face in his neck. She couldn't allow him to walk back into her life after creating a tornado that had upended her psyche and torn through her heart. He had to work a little harder than that.

She tipped her head to the side. 'That's it? Is that all you've got?'

'No,' Ben told her as he slipped off his coat and threw it over the back of her couch. It looked, damn him, as though it belonged there. He looked as though he belonged in her flat, as though it was a space he'd always been part of. She'd felt the same when she was in his house in Reykjavik, completely at home, as though the house had been waiting for her arrival to make it complete.

Ben came to stand next to her, close enough for her to smell his heady cologne. But he didn't touch her and she was grateful. If he did, she might just shatter.

'I was stupid to run out of your life, to give up on what we had. I was scared. Love, being in love, is a scary business, Mils.'

Hearing him admit his fears made hers recede. Just a little. 'I'm scared, too, Ben. But not so scared that I'd prefer a life without you to one with you in it.'

The tip of his index finger ran down her cheek, along her jaw. 'At the Harpa Concert Hall, I started to tell you that I wanted more than a December fling and I felt overcome with emotion. Then I tried to speak and my words wouldn't come. That petrified me.'

'You managed to keep arguing with me just fine,' Millie pointed out. She'd told him that the night they argued, but her words hadn't sunk in.

'I finally, with a little help, realised that,' he admitted, his hand cupping the back of her neck. 'Olivier helped me understand that my stuttering was a minor blip, not a complete meltdown.'

She narrowed her eyes at him, needing to make sure he heard her words and took them seriously. 'I said it a few nights ago and I'll say it again... I don't care if you stutter occasionally, I don't care if you stutter *all* the time. I'm in love with you and my love is *not* conditional.'

Ben rested his forehead on hers and closed his eyes. 'You don't know how much I needed to hear that, Mils.'

'But do you believe me?'

He opened his eyes, nodded, and Millie caught the sheen of emotion in his deep blue eyes. 'I— I really do.'

She swiped her lips across his, but pulled back before she got distracted. 'You have to talk to me,

Ben, I need you to let me in. I can't be the only one talking all the time.'

He kissed her forehead, left his lips there before pulling back. When his eyes met hers, she saw capitulation in his. 'I know. I promise to work on that, but you've got to keep reminding me.'

She touched his jaw with her fingertips. 'Okay.'

Millie was happy to see his eyes were a lighter blue. He stroked her hair off her face before rubbing the back of his neck. 'If our kid has a stutter...you won't blame me?'

Our and *kid* in the same sentence... Millie thought her heart would burst with happiness. 'If *our* child stutters, we'll get him the best help possible, as early as possible. And we'll never let him think there's anything wrong with him,' she told him, sounding a little fierce. 'Because there is *absolutely* nothing wrong with you, there never has been.'

Ben's emotion-filled grin was a little crooked. 'We might have a girl, you know.'

She'd always been so certain she'd have a boy, but now she didn't care. 'I will take any gender you give me, Ben.'

He brushed his lips with hers in a kiss so tender it closed her throat, just a little. 'I love you so much, Millie. I can't contemplate a world without you in it,' he admitted.

All the tension of the past few days drained out of her. 'Good, because I've been miserable without you. Don't ever leave me again, Ben.'

'I promise I won't. And I hope you know that you can trust what I say, sweetheart.'

She did. He was the only man she'd ever trusted. She couldn't wait for the rest of their lives. She returned his kiss, winding her arms around his neck. Lovely minutes, or hours later, she pulled back and tipped her head back to send him a loving smile. 'Can I ask you a question?'

He brushed her hair back and swiped his thumb over her bottom lip. 'No,' he told her, a small grin touching his mouth.

She frowned, puzzled. 'Why can't I ask you a question?' she demanded.

His smile grew bigger. 'So far in our relationship, you've asked me to marry you and to give you a baby, and to sleep with you. I would like to be the one, just once, to ask a big question.'

'And what might that be?' she asked, her heart accelerating to warp speed.

'Well, I wanted to know if you'd marry me...' he softly said, love in his eyes. And at that moment, Millie saw her future in front of her, loving and being loved by this man. The money and the lavish lifestyle meant nothing—having Ben to support her, to love, and to do the same for him, was all she needed.

'We've been married a long time already, Ben,' she pointed out.

'In name only. I want to do everything we didn't do before, starting with the big engagement party, the church wedding, and the lavish reception.' His eyes held hers, as serious as a heart attack. 'I'll make a speech, Mils. I don't care what I sound like, as long as you hear how much I love you and how happy I am to make you mine.'

Although she was touched he was prepared to put himself in a highly charged, emotional situation for her, she knew she was his world and she didn't need him to prove it.

And she didn't need fancy, she just needed him. She shook her head. 'I don't need the big wedding and the fancy reception, Ben. I just need *you*.'

'What if we wrote our vows and said them under the Northern Lights?' he asked.

'Naked and in a hot pool?' she asked, laughing at him.

'It's an option, but I'd still like to see you in a wedding dress, with flowers in your hair. I want to put a ring on your finger in front of a few guests.'

So, not naked then. But, yes, that sounded completely perfect to her. 'I *love* that idea.'

'I'm so happy you are going to be my *wife*, sweetheart,' Ben murmured, pulling her into his body and burying his face in her hair. She felt his tremors and hugged him tight, knowing he needed to be loved as much as she did. They'd be fine, they had each other.

After a long, long hug, followed by an even longer kiss, Millie pulled back again. 'I was going to ask you to do something for me, Benedikt.'

'Anything.' He lifted his eyebrows and waited.

'Will you take me back to Iceland so that we can spend Christmas there? I feel that's where we need to be tonight, in the city where it all started.'

He nodded, smiling. Millie sighed, relieved. 'That was easy, I thought you'd insist on us going to bed first,' she said. To be honest, she was just the tiniest bit put out he hadn't.

His smile widened. 'There's a bedroom on the plane,' he told her, laughing. Then his eyes widened in mock horror. 'But no condoms, I'm afraid.'

She laughed, delighted at his willingness to embrace the future and give her the family they both wanted. 'I think I can deal,' she told him, love washing over her.

She didn't mind if it took ten weeks or ten years to have a baby, this man was the centre of her world. As long as she had him, she had her family.

'Let's go home, Ben.'

* * * * *

Were you swept away by the passion of
A Nine-Month Deal with Her Husband?
Then you'll be sure to love these other stories
by Joss Wood!

The Powerful Boss She Craves
The Twin Secret She Must Reveal
The Nights She Spent with the CEO
The Baby Behind Their Marriage Merger
Hired for the Billionaire's Secret Son

Available now!

#4169 THE BABY HIS SECRETARY CARRIES
Bound by a Surrogate Baby
by Dani Collins
Faced with a hostile takeover, tycoon Gio must strengthen his claim on the Casella family company with a fake engagement. He'll never commit to a real one again. Despite his forbidden attraction, his dedicated PA, Molly, is ideal to play his adoring fiancée. The only problem? Molly's pregnant!

#4170 THE ITALIAN'S PREGNANT ENEMY
A Diamond in the Rough
by Maisey Yates
Billionaire Dario's electric night with his mentor's daughter Lyssia was already out-of-bounds. But six weeks later, she drops the bombshell that she's pregnant! Growing up on the streets of Rome, Dario fought for his safety, and he is determined to make his child equally safe. There is just one solution—marrying his enemy!

#4171 WEDDING NIGHT IN THE KING'S BED
by Caitlin Crews
Innocent Helene is unprepared for the wildfire that awakens at the sight of her convenient husband, King Gianluca San Felice. And she is undone by the craving that consumes them on their wedding night. But outside the royal bedchamber, Gianluca remains ice-cold—dare Helene believe their chemistry is enough to bring this powerful ruler to his knees?

#4172 THE BUMP IN THEIR FORBIDDEN REUNION
The Fast Track Billionaires' Club
by Amanda Cinelli
Former race car driver Grayson crashes Izzy's fertility appointment to reveal his late best friend's deceit before it's too late. He always desired Izzy, but their reunion unlocks something primal in Grayson. Knowing she feels it too compels the cynical billionaire to make a scandalous offer: *he'll* give her the family she wants!

HPCNMRA1223

#4173 HIS LAST-MINUTE DESERT QUEEN
by Annie West
Determined to save her cousin from an unwanted marriage, Miranda daringly kidnaps the groom-to-be, Sheikh Zamir. She didn't expect him to turn the tables and demand she become his queen instead—and now, he has all the power...

#4174 A VOW TO REDEEM THE GREEK
by Jackie Ashenden
The dying wish of Elena's adoptive father is to be reunited with his estranged son, Atticus. Whatever it takes, she must track down the reclusive billionaire. When she finally finds him, she's completely unprepared for the wildfire raging between them. Or for his father's unexpected demand that they marry!

#4175 AN INNOCENT'S DEAL WITH THE DEVIL
Billion-Dollar Fairy Tales
by Tara Pammi
When Yana Reddy's former stepbrother walks back into her life, his outrageous offer has her playing with fire! Nasir Hadeed will clear all her debts *if* she helps look after his daughter for three months. It's a dangerous deal—she's been burned by him before, and he remains the innocent's greatest temptation...

#4176 PLAYING THE SICILIAN'S GAME OF REVENGE
by Lorraine Hall
When Saverina Parisi discovers her engagement is part of fiancé Teo LaRosa's ruthless vendetta against her family's empire, her hurt is matched only by her need to destroy the same enemy. She'll play along and take pleasure in testing his patience. But Saverina doesn't expect their burning connection to evolve into so much more...

HPCNMRB1223

Get 3 FREE REWARDS!

We'll send you 2 FREE Books plus a FREE Mystery Gift.

FREE
Value Over
$20

Both the **Harlequin® Desire** and **Harlequin Presents®** series feature compelling novels filled with passion, sensuality and intriguing scandals.

YES! Please send me 2 FREE novels from the Harlequin Desire or Harlequin Presents series and my FREE gift (gift is worth about $10 retail). After receiving them, if I don't wish to receive any more books, I can return the shipping statement marked "cancel." If I don't cancel, I will receive 6 brand-new Harlequin Presents Larger-Print books every month and be billed just $6.30 each in the U.S. or $6.49 each in Canada, a savings of at least 10% off the cover price, or 3 Harlequin Desire books (2-in-1 story editions) every month and be billed just $7.83 each in the U.S. or $8.43 each in Canada, a savings of at least 12% off the cover price. It's quite a bargain! Shipping and handling is just 50¢ per book in the U.S. and $1.25 per book in Canada.* I understand that accepting the 2 free books and gift places me under no obligation to buy anything. I can always return a shipment and cancel at any time by calling the number below. The free books and gift are mine to keep no matter what I decide.

Choose one: ☐ **Harlequin Desire**
(225/326 BPA GRNA)

☐ **Harlequin Presents Larger-Print**
(176/376 BPA GRNA)

☐ **Or Try Both!**
(225/326 & 176/376
BPA GRQP)

Name (please print)

Address   Apt. #

City   State/Province   Zip/Postal Code

Email: Please check this box ☐ if you would like to receive newsletters and promotional emails from Harlequin Enterprises ULC and its affiliates. You can unsubscribe anytime.

Mail to the **Harlequin Reader Service:**
IN U.S.A.: P.O. Box 1341, Buffalo, NY 14240-8531
IN CANADA: P.O. Box 603, Fort Erie, Ontario L2A 5X3

Want to try 2 free books from another series! Call 1-800-873-8635 or visit www.ReaderService.com.

*Terms and prices subject to change without notice. Prices do not include sales taxes, which will be charged (if applicable) based on your state or country of residence. Canadian residents will be charged applicable taxes. Offer not valid in Quebec. This offer is limited to one order per household. Books received may not be as shown. Not valid for current subscribers to the Harlequin Presents or Harlequin Desire series. All orders subject to approval. Credit or debit balances in a customer's account(s) may be offset by any other outstanding balance owed by or to the customer. Please allow 4 to 6 weeks for delivery. Offer available while quantities last.

Your Privacy—Your information is being collected by Harlequin Enterprises ULC, operating as Harlequin Reader Service. For a complete summary of the information we collect, how we use this information and to whom it is disclosed, please visit our privacy notice located at corporate.harlequin.com/privacy-notice. From time to time we may also exchange your personal information with reputable third parties. If you wish to opt out of this sharing of your personal information, please visit readerservice.com/consumerschoice or call 1-800-873-8635. **Notice to California Residents**—Under California law, you have specific rights to control and access your data. For more information on these rights and how to exercise them, visit corporate.harlequin.com/california-privacy.

HDHP23